Dr. Mark Flint scowled as he and his mother suffered through their conversation about his brother. He had gotten into some trouble and had been caught doing drugs. Of course, they had insisted on a drug test and had lost his job. This was a job that he arranged for his brother four years ago. Paul was a 34 year old single man who seemed hell-bent on ending up in jail. He was he and always getting into trouble never wanted to settle down. I always have to bail that leech out and get him back on his feet. 'It never FAILS!' Mark fumed inwardly.

He was glad Lisa and the kids were gone on her book tour with her so that they would not feel ashamed for their uncle being busted again for drugs. But here was his mother saving his ass and asking Mark to give him another job and give him another chance to help him finally learn his lesson. But Mark knew that Paul would never learn his lesson until he until he chose to.

"Knock knock!"

"Come in Mom, come in, and have a seat and tell me all that happened."

His mother, Martha Flint, walked in with her usual fake smile she used when having to share another 'Paul had a party' story. She sat down in one of the chairs and put her purse to the side and began her plea for Paul

"Paul and Britney went out the night before to the movies and for some reason ended up at Britney's cousin's house who had just got out of jail for pushing marijuana."

"How old is Britney?"

"She's 23 and a sophomore in community college."

"Why does he date sexy young girls, ones that are related to drug pushers? He's 34 years old for Christ's sake!"

Mark did not want to lay into his mother with his angry tone.

"What else happened?"

His mother shifted uneasily in her chair. "Mark, he had marijuana and cocaine in his blood and he forgot that he had a drug test the next day. They fired him. There is also a rumor that he had been caught hacking to two days before which was the reason why they wanted to do the drug test. When Britney found out she dumped him and kicked him out of her apartment so he's back with me in his old room and I am personally delighted to see him and have him around. "

Mark sighed.

"Where is he now?"

"He's outside talking to your secretary Jenny probably trying to get her to go out with him."

"Oh, that's just great maybe he can finally meet a girl and get her pregnant so he can have an extra mouth to feed."

"He is your younger brother and we only have each other. You, me, and Paul. I will not have bad blood tear us apart. We are here hoping that you can give him a job here at the medical center."

Mark shuffled some papers and looked.

"We do have a few openings however, I don't know if I can trust him in an important computer position."

"It's what he's good at. You know that he is a whiz with computers. Just before he quit college he had a 3.6 GPA and had already helped build the community college's computer internet. You can do the same for your psych center here at the hospital." Martha's eyes pleaded with Mark to give Paul one more chance.

"Yes, Mom, but he was also fired from that position when they found out he was using the computer system to break into cameras in the girl's locker rooms. I never said anything but I think Paul may have problems with sex and sex addiction. That would not bode well here at our state-run Psychology Center here in Knoxville."

"Please Mark, please find something for him."

Mark sighed again.

"Bring him in here."

His mom got up and walked to the .door she saw him sitting on Jenny's desk looking down at her and flirting. "So, you come here often..?"

"Paul?" Martha interrupted frowning.

He pretended to not hear her. 'Mom should know I'm getting my game on.' He thought.

"Paul Matthew Flint, you answer me when I speak to you."

Paul rolled his eyes with his back to his mother but looking at Jenny.

"Yes, Mommy dearest, I'll be right there."

He got up and strode right into his brother's office .

"Hello Markee."

Mark scowled at his brother.

"You know you're acting like a teenager, right? Could you show some adult characteristics today?"

"Oh Mark, you act too serious. So what's up mom says that you can give me a job here with computers?"

Irritated, Mark began to read the letter he received from HR.

"Dr. Flint, we have three positions available. We have a night shift orderly position available, we have a day shift computer assistant, and we also have a day shift computer supervisor position available. If at any time you have find someone that can fill these positions, please let us know as we are desperate here for help."

His mother smiled, "Oh that's a blessing! So when will he start computer supervisor position?"

Dr. Flint settled himself in his chair for the fight he knew was coming.

"I'm not giving him the computer supervisor position mother."

Both the visitors sat absolutely still as if struck.

"What do you mean you're not giving me the computer supervisor position?" Paul barked angrily.

"Because, Paul, I can't trust you to stick around long enough to maintain an intricate computerized hospital infrastructure that needs 24-7 hour care."

"Are you saying I'm not trustworthy?"

"Yes, that's exactly what I'm saying."

"So you're going to stay here and teach me a lesson about life and responsibilities and character?"

"Yep."

"So you're just not going to give me a job at all, you're going to make me go out and find something else right?"

"Oh no, I can give you a job no problem but I'm pretty sure you're not going to like the job that I gave you."

Paul's face wrinkled up in anger.

"Oh I see you're going to give me the other job."

"Well, Paul, you're starting to read my mind. Yes I'm thinking about giving you the orderly job."

"I'm not going to be an orderly cleaning up crazy peoples s*** and piss or being punched shot stabbed or puked on."

Not flinching, Mark stood his ground.

"I tell you what, Paul, if you do the orderly job for 6 months to a year and show me that you can be reliable and trustworthy and show up to work I'll put you in a computer supervision position."

Their mother jumped in the conversation.

"This sounds reasonable. Son, you have been acting like a brat. Mark has to take care of these people and their lives depend on him. Also if you do not take this job, you cannot live with me, you'll have to find another place to live."

Paul looked at both of them angrily. "We both know I need this job in order to get Britney back."

"I don't give a damn about your hooch," Mark retorted. "You are not going to be bringing drug addicts to our mother's house."

Paul stood up and walked out of the room slamming Mark's office door.

Mark looked at his mother blankly.

"Have him here on Monday he can have all the tests ran and all the papers completed. "He'll be on the night shift."

His mother sighed.

"Okay, I'll get all the paperwork and everything set up if you will we'll have him start within a week."

"That I can do but Mom I'm going to be watching him like a hawk. He'll be out on his ass if he screws this up."

She sighed as she got up and walked to the door. Her sons were complete opposite of each other. They both had good hearts, but clearly her eldest had more discipline than her younger son had. He only employed discipline when he was mixing drinks or loading up bong pipes.

She just hoped Pauley, her curly haired baby, would realize he wasn't getting any younger. He seemed to mirror her ex-husband's personality to a T.


Paul and his mother sat quietly as she drove them back home.

"Do you think I'm worthless?" Paul really did not want his mom to think he was a loser.

"No sweetie, I think deep down you are confused and sad and a little bit bored with life."

"At 34 though? I mean it just doesn't seem like there's anything for me."

His mother sighed. "That's not true! You are just as smart as your brother. Maybe you haven't had the same opportunities but you've never wanted to be a psychologist."

Paul talked looking away from his mom's face. His voice sunk into sad depressive tones his mother could notice.

"I just feel like there's nothing in life that is for me. Nothing works right for me I can't seem to find a good girl either."

"Britney isn't a good girl she's 23 and she's barely out of high school." his mother added.

"She dumped me anyway."

His Mother looked at him with a tear in her eye.

"You can do much better than that trash, Paul. Just give this job chance, Sweetie."

They grew silent as she pulled up into her driveway.

He leaned over and planted a kiss on her cheek.

"It'll be okay Mom."

Tears flowed from her eyes as she watched him walk into the house. It had been she and her boys for such a long time. Her eldest boy was the embodiment of success, psychologist, husband, father. He kept the family together and took care of his mother and Paul. But as Paul reached adulthood, he seem to pale under Mark's shadow.

"I hope he can find himself before it's too late."

## 2

First night of work went really slow most of his work consisted of meeting his coworkers learning his schedule and running the idiosyncrasies of these patients that were now in his care. He noticed majority of the patients were older except for two one man in his late forties was there for observation after having killed his wife and children in a fit of insane rage.

The other patient was a younger woman in her late thirties that looks even younger. She spent most of her time with lease an elderly lady and that had been diagnosed with severe depression and the beginnings of dementia. Paul didn't have much to do with the patients directly in those first few weeks but he did find younger woman very attractive.

He had been given this spiel about interaction with the patients at the hospital Carol had told him the story about Edward the previous swirly that was caught trying to molest the younger female patient. He had been caught trying to the female patient in the shower only to be attacked by Jack and stabbed repeatedly from jealousy. She mentioned that Jack had transferred all of his jealousy to this younger girl who he had replaced as his wife in his mind. Elise took the younger girl under her wing and looks out for heaths her own daughter. He was also told that meaning or separate during shower times and a few of those he had to be in there with them as they showered. He felt a little bit of fear at possibly getting hurt by these crazy people. Resentment grew in his throat every time he thought of his brother giving him this s***** job to teach him a lesson.

Ugh, he thought as he scanned in the building Carol and Joe will be leaving at 1:30 it only be home until 7:13 in the morning. 'Got to get these crazy people clean', he thought.

At 11 pm, he went with Joe to go take them into the shower stalls for night-time showers everything what gone smoothly until Carol and the ladies came for shower time. One of the older patients had passed out and had vomited all over the floor on the way back to their room and Jack had escaped and ran back into the shower rooms and had accosted the younger female patient. Paul was the only one that went after him and was able to wrestle him off of the girl. She had fallen to the bottom of the shower while he dealt with Jack. He slapped the wall alarm and yelled for help when Carol and Joe had bursting in bearing meds.

Carol quickly gave Jack a shot in the rear. Paul looked frantically around in and sat the woman up. He had a hard time not looking at her breasts reminding himself that she was crazy and dangerous.

"What do I need to do Carol?"

Carol looked up frantically at Paul and the young woman.

"Annika appears to have gone catatonic again normally we don't have the male orderlies taking care of the females but could you finish washing her and take her back to her room we are short staffed tonight and it will take me Joe few others to settle Jack back down."

Paul looked back at Annika. She wasn't moving.

"Is she going to wake up Carol?"

Wrestling Jack up on his feet, Carol yelled back,

"She might be awake tomorrow but don't be surprised if it's 3 or 4 days."

He picked her up on her feet. "Okay Annika, let's get you clean and tucked in bed."

He took a wash rag and soap and washed every inch of her body. Since her hair was up he decided not to wash it with shampoo. He put her arm around his shoulder and rinsed her off with the removable shower spray.

'You're a very pretty, pretty girl, Annika.' He thought, as he wrapped a towel around her and lifted her up to carry her back to her room. He walked quietly as he carried her and laid her on her bed. He went through her clothes in the drawer and grabbed a pair of panties noticing that they were stacked in a certain order of color. He grabbed the yellow panties he saw and put them on her then began looking for a sleep shirt. Dammit, he thought I bet all of her shirts are being washed. He looked back at her exposed breasts he took off his shirt put it on her.

"That should do until we get your clothes. I'll go and get them right now you just go ahead and sleep tight Miss Annika."

He walked lightly out of her room and closed the door. She opened her eyes as the door clicked shut.

Paul sat down with Carol in the staff lounge.

"Carol, who is Annika and why is she here?"

Sitting back in her chair she began to tell him about Annika and her stay there at the psych ward. "Annika is a sweetheart and she is very beautiful. She sometimes helps us when we're short-staffed too. She is very intelligent. Where ever she's from I have a feeling that her family is gone. She's 38."

"38? I would have guessed 28."

"She does look younger but she is 38. It's that blonde hair and brown eyes. I was told that she was brought here suicidal due to bipolar issues but I have really never seen that. I've never seen her have a meltdown. This place is top-of-the-line with your brother running it so someone with money put her in here. She may be Hispanic cause I've caught her singing in Spanish."

"What happened with the previous orderly?"

"They say he got obsessed with her. He said that she came on to him and promised him sex for things. He says it's her fault that Jack is jealous over any other guy that talks to her he implied that she had sexual relations with Jack. But I don't think so. She never goes down the male lock up corridor alone and we keep them on stricter schedule. She spends all of her time with Elise and usually only see him at recreation-time before dinner and like what happened last night maybe at shower time."

"How long have you been here Carol?"

"I've been here for 12 years your brother is very good at working with these people and so is your sister-in-law. They'd actually help people get out of here and lead normal lives and he always takes care of staff workers who stay. What was he like growing up?"

Paul laughed. 'Stiff as a board' he thought. "No, Mark is a lot like my mom, she was a veterinarian and taking all kinds of strays and helped people's pets get better. Only Mark does it with people. They took care of me pretty good specially after our father abandoned us."

"He sure found gold when he found Lisa."

"Yes she is, she's very good lady. I was kind of hoping that I would find my Lisa when I was in college but it never happened. I was afraid that there was something wrong with me."

"Abandoned you?"

"Yes Carol, he laughed, he literally ran off with the secretary. We haven't seen him since."

"I'm sorry to hear that."

"Don't be, mother took care of us and put us both through college."

"Have you paid her back?"

"In hugs and kisses, no, I should though. Mark has."

"You should, Paul. You come from good people."

"Carol got up and stretched. You seem to know your way around here you are doing pretty good so far."

"Oh it's just the blind leading the blind, Carol."

She laughed "And you're funny and that's exactly what we need here".

3

Lisa needs to get home, pronto, Mark grumbled. He found himself waking up from a nap since 2:30 now it was 5. Lisa went to get the kids from school and must have stopped at the store. He had been feeling the loneliness since she and the kids had been gone on her book tour. With running the hospital, his brother, and his family had little time to rest.

He missed seeing his naked wife's body next to him in bed. She always seemed to be perfect relaxation method that he always needed to unwind. Of course, all that has changed after the kids were born. He listened carefully for the familiar catering in the door opening of his house and with a relaxed sigh hoping that she had returned home finally.

"Alright, I went and got you guys something from Burger King when I want you guys to do now is to take out your homework finish it up and then you guys can watch Netflix for the rest of the night and till 10:30 let me go check on your father he's been home since 2." She declared. "The last thing we need is a stomach pestilence to ravage our home again." She muttered under her breath.

He laughed as he heard her sarcasm through the walls. She came into the room so relaxing I see, you do know tomorrow is your day with the children.

"Oh Lisa, they're good kids. You're a great mother they do what you tell them to."

"How are they going to go wrong with psychologists for parents?"

She jumped on the bed with him and began rubbing his chest. "How are our other kids?" She smiled sweetly.

"Paul started at the hospital a few weeks ago."

"How do you think he's going to do, Mark? He always seems to remind me of someone with mild depression."

"I noticed that too. He covers it well with the jokes he tells. But yes, there is depression."

"He's not the type that would hurt himself is he?"

"Maybe if he were older and he felt like he was going nowhere with his life. But right now I don't think he's at that point."

She rolled off the bed and started taking off her clothes talk to me while I'm taking a shower cause I can tell there is more on your mind.

He watched her walking to the bathroom and turn on the shower.

"It's just that I think there's an addiction problem but I can't find out if it's drugs or if it's sex it may be just chronic laziness. He is a very talented man with computers that supervisor position but if he never comes in on Mondays and Tuesdays from getting as drunk on the weekends, then there's no point in even hiring him."

Lisa yelled above the sound of the shower. "But I thought you already hired him."

"Yes as an orderly."

"You sure that was smart Mark? I love your brother but do you think he has what it takes to be an orderly."

"First impulse says no second impulse says maybe. He gets along with his coworkers they like him a lot and he has shown up to work on time in the last two weeks."

"Well, that's promising."

Mark walked into the bathroom and watched her shower this is always been better than porn he thought. He caught her last couple of words

"…….. You want me to talk to him and say something?"

"Nah I'll keep on top of this." He took his clothes off and walked into the shower stall with her.

"So this is why you took a nap this afternoon."

"I just can't fool you can I, Lisa?"

"But we can't make too much noise this time."

"We should have dropped them off at their grandmother's house."

He began to feel all of her creases of her body and ended at her heaving breasts.

"It's a good thing I've already washed my body."

"I'm just here making sure you did it right."

"Ha ha, that's what they all say. Sounds like you want to make me dirty again."

"So she admits she's a dirty girl everyone, finally."

Lisa laughed turning to face him. I am going to hire a professional washer know anybody

"Who should I turn my resume into?"

Lisa laughed as she pulled his head down to kiss him. This time you get handcuffed.

He picked up her left leg and pinned her to the shower wall. "You'll have to handcuff me because this will wear us both out and laying on my back with you on top is the way to go."

Lisa rolled her eyes as they kissed. The shower hid the loud moans from the rest of the house.

## 4

Lisa slept naked against Mark's chest later on that night.

"Oh I was going to tell you I bumped into Dr. John Driscoll on my book tour last week. I asked him about Annika. And he said he'd never heard of her. I said yes we receive papers that Annika Garcia was being transferred from Johnson State mental health facility in Pittsburgh Pennsylvania. He said he doesn't call any woman by that name. I'm going to do some digging and find out what's going on Annika doesn't seem like the crazy type to be committed to a hospital."

Mark thought hard about the woman. "She does appear quite competent I need to talk to her again anyway. It seems like Jack has picked her to be his emotional replacement for his murdered wife he's tried several times to attack her and force himself on her."

"Has she made any violent attacks against anyone?"

"Not that I'm aware. She has become very close to an elderly lady called Elise."

"Elise, demented naked old lady?"

"The very one." He remarked.

Mark had a worried look. "You be careful when you're digging around in things like this remember what happened to the guy 5 years ago who was actually in Witness Protection and the criminals came looking for him….."

"Don't worry! I have my resources I also have friends in low places tell me find all the information that I need without having it traced back to me."

"Well right now I'm going to have to talk to Paul and see how everything is going with him. I'm going to need to keep an eye on him to make sure he doesn't burn the whole place down."

Lisa laughed. "Well he is a Flint."

Mark turned out the light and pulled her close.

"Not the best Flint."

Paul was there at his office bright and early at 8 o'clock in the morning. It took in for a surprise that he was there since Paul rarely crawled out of the bed before 12 noon.

"So what do you think of the madhouse so far?"

"It's not as bad as I thought it would be."

"Well I'm really shocked. Most people rarely last 2 weeks. So tell me what you think of the patients."

"Whoa."

"Yes call these are really sick people."

"I didn't think they would be that violent. Well Jack is the only one that I've seen attack anyone."

"Did he attack Annika?"

"Yes she seems really scared of him and very fragile."

"She does but I do want to warn you just because they appear weak and fragile does not mean that they are. None of the patients have asked you for favors have they?"

"Yeah but what do you mean by favors."

"Some of the patients will try to get to do things for you for you to do things for them."

"What could these patients do for me."

"Well some of the women do try to solicit themselves for sex."

"You do realize that most of these women are over the age of 50 right? Well except for Annika."

"I am serious and yes they would and yes you should be wary of Annika too the last orderly was stabbed by Jack because he thought he and Anna were having sex."

"Why is he here? He doesn't seem to fit this place."

"I took him as a favor of the governor. For the most part, he stays separated from the rest of the patients so that reduces any of the fights."

"Did she sleep with Jack?"

"I don't know. It's possible but he comes with a lot of baggage from what happened with his family he could very well be projecting."

"Is she on birth control?"

"Not that I know of."

"Well you're her doctor, why don't you prescribe birth control? What if she does get raped or sexually assaulted you wouldn't want her to get pregnant, would you?"

"Well, I guess you're right I've been slowly taking her off of the strict med s that she was prescribed to keep her under control. I'm hoping to get Lisa to talk to her to find out more about her."

Paul sat quietly before speaking again. "Are we done here so everything's good with us?"

Mark looked at him intently. "Are you doing okay Paul? Anything going on with you that you'd like to talk about?"

Paul stood up and headed towards the door. "No Marco, but thanks for asking." He stopped to flash a goofy grin of his brother.

"Good luck, Paul."

Paul decided to come to work about 4 hours early to see the patient's free time and at dinner. Carol smiled as she watched him walk into the common area.

"Sounds like you love it here, Mr. Flint."

He laughed. "Actually, Carol, I want to get a better idea of who these patients are and what I'm up against when I'm here by myself."

Carol snickered. "They can be just as wild at day time as they are at nighttime."

Paul looked around and saw everyone but Jack. Carol read his mind and told him aloud what he was thinking.

"Jack eats in his room. We can't afford him stabbing other people and trying to kill other patients other institutions would feel like they were violating his rights by keeping him contained but your father tends to hold her more strict point of view on maintaining peace and calm wood violent patients."

Paul looked around the cafeteria and he made eye contact with Annika.

She had a small smile for him but then immediately turned away to Elise to listen to what she had to say.

"Have you heard anything else about Annika, Carol? How has she been doing?"

"She's been doing great yes when she's away from Jack. When we separate him out from this crowd, everyone does well. I know I'm harping too much on Jack but I really want you to be careful because he is dangerous and he would be jealous of you."

"I can watch my back, Carol. Has Annika ever been violent?"

"Nope not yet I really think she may be in here by mistake but then you never know she could have a breakdown and we will never I seen it coming."

Before she could finish talking, someone came running down the corridor to the cafeteria. Jack had a knife and was out running the other orderlies trying to hunt down Annika. He found her and grabbed her by the neck with a knife to her throat in the corner. Elise was screaming begging the orderlies to talk him out of his jealous rage and anger.

"Let her go, Jack."

"This b**** cheated on me with my best friend she's going to die!" Jack looked wild eyed and ready to stab Paul.

"She is not your wife, Jack, remember you already killed your wife and kids."

"No!" He was swaying and jerking more.

Paul tried to reason with Jack noticing that Annika was losing breath and was about to pass out.

"Someone call Mark and grab a full round of Thorazin meds. Jack, Dr. Flint is coming. If he sees you holding Annika that way going to have to ship you to another facility away from here. Let Annika go and you go back to your room."

"Who the f*** are you?" Screamed Jack.

"I'm Paul Flint, Dr. Flint's brother, and I'm here to help you."

"No you are the son of a b**** trying to steal my wife!!!"

Paul remarked "Well if I am then that knife belongs to me, try sticking it in me."

Jack threw Annika to the side and lunged at Paul. Elise, enmeshed in fear and confusion, leaped to stop Jack but took a full knife stab in her heart. Annika screamed as everyone watch the Elise collapsed to the ground with a knife in her chest. Paul tackled Jack and wrestled him to the ground with his arms behind his back. Carol rushed to Elise.

Carol gasped. "She's dying. Go take Annika to her room. This experience could really mess her up. They both looked up at her lying in a catatonic position on the floor as vacant and limp.

"You sure you don't need my help Carol?"

"Your brother's going to be here soon. Just take Annika to her room. If that poor child was normal before she won't be after this experience."

Paul walked over to her. He picked Annika up and carried her down to her room. 'She really was a beautiful woman' Paul said to himself. When he arrived he tenderly placed her on the bed she began to rouse from the shock she had just experienced and began to scream and thrash about but held her down to the bed to keep from hurting herself. His hand fell on her breast and she looked into his eyes. He gave into an impulse.

"Maybe I can do something for you to help you calm you down."

Slowly he slid his hands into her sweatpants until he found her wet. With his hands on her he slowly rubbed her increasing in intensity and she began to moan. She grabbed his arm as her orgasm started to rack her body. Her moans grew louder to his intensity and she let out scream of pleasure. He began to bring her down from her orgasm to help her catch her breath. His manhood was erect and she noticed she began to come down from her high.

"There that should at least give you a little bit of stress relief.

The eased his hands out of her sweatpants and stood up. In a breathy voice, she whispered a very weak thank you.

He grabbed her pinky finger and smile and then walked out of her room. She laid there and drenched in sweat thinking about his blue eyes. Paul spent the rest of his night in a fog. He couldn't get Annika out of his brain. Her eyes and her pale skin in the pale moonlight intoxicated him.

He found himself walking to her room after he had made his rounds with everyone else he kept trying to come up with a reason for being there quietly he slipped into her room and watched her figure underneath the blanket.

"Annika." He whispered

She opened her eyes and turn to face him in the moonlight. She laid there looking up at him with big eyes.

He reached down and touched her cheek he finally sat down and pulled up her shirt to expose her breasts. His fingertips lightly touched her nipples making them hard.

In one swift motion, he leaned down and kissed her full on the lips. Then leaning back to see her reaction he then stood up and took his shirt off he pulled back her blankets and then joined her in the bed. He held her hands down as he removed her top slowly undressing her. She shivered as she felt the cool air on her naked skin.

"I need you." He groaned slightly

He separated her legs and pushed himself fast inside of her as if afraid that she would say no.

She began to moan loudly. Her moans intensified the faster he pushed inside of her he held her hand softly linking his fingers in between hers.

In 15 minutes, it was over. Both were bathed in sweat. He kissed her cheek he stood back up and begin to put his clothes on he stared at her face as he pulled the blanket over her body Then he tucked her in her bed.

"Sleep." he whispered.

He turned and walked out of her room she closed her eyes trying to remember every sensation.

The rest of the night he spent in a haze.

## 5

Carol was the first to notice Annika was acting strange when Paul signed in the next day. She reported that Annika seemed more lighthearted than usual.

"Really Paul, she's acting like a very intelligent young adult and not a debilitated person."

"Carol, I don't think she has a mental disability or a mental health issue person. I think she's just a normal person that's had some hard circumstances.

"That may be true I spoke to your brother about her she said that your sister-in-law is doing an investigation somehow the previous hospital does not have any record of her ever having been there."

"Has she ever said anything?"

"Nope, nothing."

They walked into the cafeteria where he saw Annika sitting on the opposite side of the room from yesterday's event. She was alone.

"What do they do with Jack?"

"Oh, he's on the first mental bus out of here he's headed to the Okapi home for the criminally insane."

"Has Annika said anything about what happened yesterday?"

"Nope, nothing either."

Paul looked at Annika, "I'm going to go talk to her really quick maybe she'll open up to me. I'll see you later.

Carol nodded," I'll see you later."

Paul walked over to where Annika was sitting quietly eating her dinner. "Hey"

She looked up with a smile. "Hey"

"How are you doing today?

"Not bad."

"I am hope I didn't hurt you last night."

She picked at her food. "Um no, you didn't."

He reached out and grabbed her pinky with his.

"I really like you Annika."

"I like you too, Mr. Flint."

"Call me Paul."

"Well I have to go and get some work done let me know if you need anything."

She watched him walk away knowing that he would probably be in her room later that night.

Mark said in his office staring at his phone, 'Oh I really need Lisa right now.' he moaned out loud. 'Someone help me get this paperwork done.'

She answered the phone after he patiently waited for the dial tone to ring.

"Hey babe, where you at?"

"I'm at the store. What's up? You are so ridiculous when you use your funny accents."

"Sometimes I just need to pretend that I'm someone else, geez Louise, I think you'd throw me a bone."

She giggled. "So you got rid of Jack Wright?"

"Yep he's off to the criminally insane bar with endless and endless shots of thorizine per crazy request."

"Good, what you need me to do?"

"Well, I need you to evaluate the employees and a few of the patients. I need to stop a problem before it happens."

"What problems?"

"Well, Annika might end up with PTSD and I need you to make sure that Paul and Carol aren't suffering from it either. I can't lose Carol she's one of my best employees."

"I guess I can finish up my writing today and then go down there tomorrow talk to them. How is Paul doing?"

"He's doing great he completely stepped in with Jack stabbed Elise Carolyn the others love him even quiet Annika is warming up to him."

"That's amazing."

"Yes I think I might make him IT supervisor in 6 months."

"Wow."

"I am worried though that Paul's going to figure out a way to screw all this up."

"How so?"

"All by doing something stupid like having meth or marijuana in his pee or getting caught sleeping with one of the patients."

"He wouldn't sleep with a crazy patient."

"You never know with Paul."

"Well Mark let's hope not. Be careful speaking things into existence." She laughed.

He sighed. "You're right."

"Hey it's Thursday, make sure you are home today by 5."

"Yes, ma'am."

"You don't want to make me mad right now. We know who's the boss around our house."

He laughed. "Don't put me on the spot like that, woman."

"Feel free to take a nap there if you need to."

"I'm going to need a nap just to keep up with you and the kids."

"What would I do without you? You make me laugh so much."

"Actually you probably be a millionaire by now or married to one."

"I doubt it. I speak too freely."

He smiled. "What time are you going to be here tomorrow?"

"Oh let's say 9:30 and you and I will go out to lunch. Joey wants to play basketball and we need to talk about that."

"Okay sounds like a plan. I'm going to talk to Paul and Carol tonight about tomorrow finish up this paper work and I will go ahead and leave here for the day. See you soon."

"Okay love you, babe."

"Love you too."

He thought, as he heard her hang up her phone, she always makes my day better. I should have picked a woman that would have nagged me to death.

Paul was daydreaming about Annika as he stood by his locker before the night shift. He found himself thinking about her even when he was at home staring at the TV screen. She was his last thought before he drifted off to sleep.

He ambled into the hallway to work that orderly station looking for Carol. After looking around he didn't see her and he has to get it working where she was.

"Where is Carol at tonight?"

"Oh she called in sick along with the stomach plague that one of her babies passed on to her."

"Ew."

"That's what I'm saying."

"She needs to keep it at her house."

"I know that's right. Hey, here's a note that you are to stand outside of the girls shower room. I think they've already started. There's only a few that are left just stand outside the door and just listen for any problems."

"She would be one of the last ones in the shower he thought. I'll head down there now."

"When you reach the shower, knock on the door."

He sauntered up to the shower room. "Hello, anyone in here?"

He heard faint singing. "It's just me, Annika." Her voice broke through the shower noise.

Paul walked towards the corner where she was showering. Her back was to him as she was washing her hair.

"Need some help?" He reached for the shower head.

"I don't think you're supposed to be in here." She stammered.

Paul smiled. "It's not like I haven't seen you naked before."

She stood there quietly he rinsed all the soap out of her hair

"Turn around."

She turned and faced him. He stared at the top of her body down to her feet. Without any warning he grabbed her and he kissed her deeply he held her up as her knees gave out

He grabbed a towel and started drying her and her hair off.

"Get dressed and I'll see you tonight."

He smiled and winked as he turned and walked back out the shower room.

It was 10:30 when he made his first round. He found her in her room with her light on and her glasses she was writing intensely in what appeared to be a diary

"What's that?"

"It's just my journal where I write everything. it helps me out. Especially things come back to me with that I remember."

"Is it things that you remember from before you were here."

"Yes, a few things that I can't seem to recall or seem to be really fuzzy."

"You've never said much about your past do you remember your family or where you from."

He noticed her face turned a little bit confused. "I know a few things I just don't know how to put them in order."

"Do you remember your family?"

"I remember faces. Her face wrinkled up in confusion.

He looked down in her diary and tried to take it from her. "Let me read what you wrote."

"NO! She wrenched it back from him.

"I want to see if you wrote anything about me."

"Not much." She had just images that were beginning to come up in her mind.

"Why not? You've wrote nothing about the dashing man in your life with the large penis?"

She laughed.

"I don't write about sex."

"Well then, you keep your diary."

"Men only think of one thing."

"Pretty much."

He looked into her eyes.

"Pretty girl like you has to have a boyfriend somewhere or husband."

She sighed "If I do, I don't remember them."

He grabbed her face and looked deeper into her eyes. She knew the talk time was over when he reached over and turned out the lights.

At about 12:30, Mark called him on his phone.

"Hey how's everything going up there tonight?"

"Pretty quiet how's everything at your house?"

"It's pretty quiet now that the kids are in bed."

I hope you didn't call me after you and Lisa just did it, he thought. Thank God he didn't catch me in Annika's room either. His mind screamed.

"So what's up boss?"

"Nothing much I'm just going to have Lisa go over there tomorrow to interview you and the patients after the incident with Jack."

"Why is that?"

"Well, there has to be an investigation."

"But everybody saw what happened, it was not like he had it planned or had help."

"I know it's just protocol. I just need you to stay later. I'll have Lisa interview you first and then you can go home."

"Hey you're not going to interview Annika too are you?"

"Well yes well she was the one that Jack was choking with the knife."

"Just don't think that's fair to her."

"Normally, I would agree but since Lisa is a licensed psychologist, she'll be in good hands."

"Okay."

"How is Annika doing from your point of view?"

Paul wasn't sure about details he should give with his relationship with Annika.

"She is talking more today. She showed me her diary. I didn't read it but she mentioned that some of her memories are coming back."

"Memories?"

"Yes."

"Huh! I'll tell Lisa. She's interested in Annika's history because we have nothing on her background to either. Let me know if she says anything else."

Mark could sense his discomfort after an awkward long pause.

"Anything else going on, bro?"

"Nothing, I'm just curious though what is the policy with employees dating each other or dating the patients."

"Employees dating each other is strongly discouraged employees dating patients is a hell no."

"I see."

"You're not dating Carol are you Paul? Because Carol is one of my best employees."

Paul laughed. "No I'm still trying to get back with Britney."

"Oh there's a smart idea right there Paul."

"Well, do you have anybody else in mind?"

"Maybe you should just get your life together first before you start a new relationship."

"That's good advice Mark I'm going to take that."

A shock of silence fell across Mark.

"You're actually listening to me?"

Paul laughed. "You're surprised?"

"Yes."

"Well I am 34 it's time for me to get my life together with or without a woman."

"Okay I actually am thinking about going ahead and promoting you to the IT supervisor. I do need somebody to fill that position no one gets any emails anymore and yesterday everything from January to June was deleted. "

"You just probably need a backup email server that has a special code in email messages."

"Exactly anyway I'm going to let you go I need to go to bed we all have a busy day tomorrow."

Paul hung his cell phone up he really had a hard time with himself thinking about him and Annika together.  He knew he would have to talk to Annika and end their relationship before it got out of hand.

Lisa scanned into the psych ward at the hospital with her husband at her side. "Why is he still so protective of me, this is my job….geez…" She rambled in her mind.

'So this is still this is a very dangerous place in his mind'….Her thoughts rationalized Mark's behavior.

'I don't know how we stayed together for so long.' She also thought she took a side glance at his profile. He was a mess in college when she met him. But he was tall dark and handsome and always showed up where she was.

He made all A's in all his classes that semester just to impress her with his intelligence but she found out later that the year previously he nearly flunked because he was drinking it very much with his frat boy pals. Her memories ran through her nostalgic mind.

"I arranged for Paul to be your first interviewee." Mark threw over his shoulder at her.

Lisa nodded "It'll be good to see him haven't seen him in a while how come he doesn't come over very much

Mark sighed. "Probably because he's been in trouble lately. He's back at Mom's house now and he's working the orderly night shift."

"I can't believe you put him on the night shift"

Mark grinned, "I know. And for some reason it's worked out great. He actually shines as an orderly."

Lisa laughed. "Flint men are very hard to figure out."

"We are different breed, baby, he pulled her next to the side and put his arm around your shoulder as he left her to their conference room."

"Wait here I'll go get Paul."

Mark found Paul talking to Carol in the employee lounge.

"Paul, Lisa is here to interview you to get the investigation started."

Paul looked up at his brother. "Conference room?" He asked

"Yes it is"

Paul turned to Carol. "I'll see you later. Let me know if anything happens."

He walked with his brother towards the conference room.

"What is the punishment for an employee and a patient having sexual relations?"

Mark looked at him quickly. "Have you seen this happen here?"

"No, no, I was just asking hypothetically?"

"The employee would be terminated and probably prosecuted …the patient would probably be transferred. Everyone in the hospital ward would be investigated from the top down."

"Oh, that serious?"

"Yes, very serious."

Mark left him at the conference door, "You can leave after the interview is over there shouldn't be any problems afterwards."

"Can I talk to Annika before I do my interview?"

"Why?"

"Just make sure if she's okay with it."

"She'll be fine with Lisa."

Paul felt uncertain about the entire situation as he walked into the room with his sister in law setting up the tape recorder.

"Pauley!"

Paul groaned at his brother's nickname since childhood.

"How are you Lisa?"

"I'm good except that your brother is put me to work."

"He is good at doing that. So what do we do here, do we start at my childhood?"

Lisa laughed. "No, we just started where all this began which Jack and what happened at that encounter in the cafeteria."

"I was kind of hoping I could tell you of how Mark's abusive childhood bullying. When are you going to talk to Annika?"

"I'm going to be talking to everyone I don't know when she'll be here she may be next or she may be the last person I don't know. And Mark wasn't that much of a bully to you." She laughed.

"Well, he did beat that time with his sweaty sock filled with used underwear. I'm scarred to this day."

Paul sat down in the chair and shifted uneasily

"So tell me when did all this start?"

Paul began with his first memories of Jack. He seemed to be strangely obsessed with Annika. Jack had ran into the shower with Annika that one time and she passed out and I had to take her back to her room

"I heard about that." Lisa said. "How did Annika react to you taking care of her?"

"She seemed fine."

"The reason I ask is because she has not really communicated much to the employees here she hasn't really even open up to Carol which I find really strange everyone even Jack had his moments with Carol."

"Yes, Carol is a saint."

Paul continued on mentioning that Jack would always stare at Annika and that he always called her his wife.

Lisa took notes as he talked.

He went on about the incident in the cafeteria check it been sitting in the corner by the window and had been staring how far until they had decided to start feeding him in his room.

The next day as they fed him and took care of his needs, he came across a knife on a food tray and then made a mad dash down the hall to Annika. He told Lisa everything he said to Jack word for word before Elise was stabbed as they were able to free Annika and restrain Jack.

Lisa looked carefully at Paul." How did that make you feel seeing a person die like that in front of you?"

"It scared me and I was very scared for Annika"

"Why?"

"I didn't want to see her dead."

"Paul, has Annika made any sexual advances to you or touch you inappropriately."

"No why would you say that?"

"Because people would think that maybe she brought this on herself and that she was trying to get anything that she could with the sexual advances or promises."

Paul began to get defensive 'Annika is not like that,' he thought. She's only amorous with me.' He smiled at the thought. " I haven't seen her making advances to anyone else."

Lisa smiled. "Calm down I agree with you I don't think she's that type of person and I don't think her issues are that deep. As a matter of fact I'm beginning to wonder why she's here I haven't been able to find any previous records of her at her previous hospital."

Paul grew quiet listening to the words that Lisa had just spoken. Annika really didn't have that many issues. Even so, he did not want Annika telling Lisa about their intimate relationship.

As he and Lisa wrapped up their interview, Lisa remarked. "You have nothing to worry about you did everything you could have done at the moment." 'Oh no, nothing to worry about.' he thought.

He opened the door and walked back toward the employee lounge. He passed Carol and Annika making their way to the conference room to be interviewed for Elise's murder. He and Annika made eye contact and he pleaded 'please do not tell anyone about us' Carol waived and he waved back to her rather awkwardly. Annika knew he was troubled. They both turned to look back at each other as he walked further down away from them.

Lisa met Annika and Carol to interview them both. Carol told her story and Annika filled in the details of when Jack grabbed her and held her throat. 'All the stories seem to match' Lisa thought 'Doesn't seem like there was anyone acting irrationally except for Jack.' She began to ask Annika deeper questions.

"Annika, do you know why you are in the psychiatric ward at the hospital?"

"I'm having a hard time remembering how I got here and why I'm here in the first place."

"What's wrong with me your memory? Can you remember your childhood?"

"Only bits and pieces, I can't seem to place moments together."

"You've been here for about 18 months. The previous Hospital stated that you were there for about 3 years. You're 38 now. So you practically lived half your thirties in a psychiatric hospital. Do you remember anything of what happened for people to want you to be admitted? Was it your family?"

"I don't think my family knows where I am. I'm from a different country. I don't feel like this is my home country."

"Mark told me that you speak a little Spanish. Do you remember any bad experiences before you came here?"

"No. none."

"Have you had any bad experiences since you been here other than with Jack any orderly Smith mistreated you. Did any doctors mistreat you?"

Annika hesitated. "No one other than Jack and the orderly that was fired. I keep to myself."

"Well, I do try to help Mark and keeping this place a safe haven for people trying to get better, Annika. We do work to try to help people get better many of our patients leave and actually become productive back in society again. We aren't going to keep you here if you don't need to be here."

"Yes, ma'am."

"Do please feel free to open up to me or Carol or the doctor. Let us know how you feel or if any memories come back or if anything we can do to help you."

Annika nodded.

"I'm going to let you go. I'll talk to you a little longer about procedures and policies here at this Hospital. I don't want to worry about you getting lost or doing anything odd."

After she left Lisa begin talking to Carol about Annika and all the drama at the hospital.

"What do you think of her Carol?"

"Despite that we work with older and more elderly people. She hasn't been giving me any problems and she's actually been helpful."

"I'm going to help Mark out and you getting her discharged eventually if we can get her memories pieces back together find out what she's doing here and find out how we can help her and I think she can be reintroduced into society."

"I agree to."

"Carol, how is Paul doing?"

"He's doing great. He hasn't choked at all the drama here. He gets along with the other employees."

"Mark was worried that he would blow this job."

"I haven't seen it.  I haven't seen him being unwilling to work he's cleaned up some nasty messages with a straight face and he's been able to."

"He works with Annika very well. She's opened up a lot."

"You don't think there's anything inappropriate between those two?" They're about the same age he's probably about 2 to 3 years younger than her.

"I haven't seen it but then I don't work night shift so……."

"I don't think so either. A relationship between her and Paul would be bad especially since he's going to be changing jobs. Paul's going to be working day shift as a computer supervisor he might not be seeing much of an Annika or any of the other patient as much as he used to."

"Will be sad to see him go but I'm sure he's glad for the desk job."

"Okay, Carol I think we're done here.  I'll give my report to the doctor and if he approves of it, he'll send it on to the state. We've sent Jack down to Chattahoochee. I'm sure he'll have some fun there with like-minded people as himself."

"I'll see you later Lisa."

Paul knew what he had to do and he dreaded doing it that night. He waited for that work phone call saying he'd had been fired for an inappropriate relationship with the patient however that phone call never came. It didn't seem to make any sense since Annika was a consenting adult.

Only one thought raced through his mind. "I have to end this now."

He showed up to work clocked in and went through the routine of getting ready for the shift he was strangely quiet and did not speak to Carol and other employee Buddies. He watched the clock until the 1 o'clock shift came and he began begin to walk down the Halls walking in securing doors. He came up to Anika's room he tapped on her door and walked in he saw her lying on the bed with her back to him return to him with a smile

"How are you?"

"I'm good and you?"

"How is the investigation?"

He picked up a chair and sat down beside her bed.

"Need to talk to you about something."

"Go ahead" She noticed his worried look.

"Did you know that it's rather illegal for an employee and a patient to have a relationship?"

"But I am a grown adult."

"Yes I know, but you are a patient."

"But I would never press charges."

"I know you wouldn't but it's still wrong I could lose my job and it could keep me from…" He almost said from seeing you. He looked into her eyes. She had beautiful deep brown eyes.

"Please don't do this," she whispered.

"Look, Annika you deserve better than this. I don't even think you need to be here do you know why you're here. Who put you in here?"

She looked away after a long pause she said. "I can't remember. One minute I was working in an office in the next minute I was strapped to a bed I just keep having these white flashes of memory and very active dreams."

"Have you told Lisa about any of this?"

"No……"

"You should talk to her"

"I don't, I don't feel comfortable sharing…anything. I'm afraid I might tell something I shouldn't and I don't know why I feel that way…."

"You can talk to me."

"No, I'm not I don't think that's a good idea." she began shifting around them for bed.

He got up out of the chair and move to the bed he leaned in and kissed her lips softly. "Get some rest." he whispered. "I'm sorry."

She looked away and comfortably he got up and walked towards the door and walked out of the room. He fought the feeling of staying with her and touching her. He spent the rest of the night racked in emotional agony and guilt.

Loneliness descended upon them both for the next couple of weeks. Annika kept to herself and they both avoid each other. Every now and then they would catch themselves looking at each other with pained looks. Not long after, Paul was reassigned to a day job by his brother as a data specialist. He never interacted with any of the patients again except for popping in to visit Carol and the other employees at lunch or after work. Carol mentioned that Annika had kind of withdrawn into herself and had watching the news is more intently especially political news of upheaval in Central America. She caught Annika staring intently at the TV and getting more upset at watching the news. One October evening, Carol expressed even more worried tone with Annika.

"Have you seen Annika?"

"No, I haven't. How is she doing?"

"She's starting to get even more anxious about what she's watching on TV."

Paul sighed. "What is she watching on TV?"

Carol grew quiet." I haven't told anyone. I've just been watching her. She doesn't act like she's one of the patients here sometimes I catch her interacting fine with me and other people but then after watching TV for a few minutes and  then I see her moving back and forth fingers in her ears. If I didn't know any better I would think that she was having flashbacks. I try to inquire about it, but she won't open up to me."

Paul was worried. 'I hope our past relationship has not thrown her into a tailspin.' He thought.

"Let me talk to her."

Carol's face wrinkled "Are you sure that Dr. Flint would want you talking to a patient?"

"It wouldn't hurt plus, um, maybe I can get her to tell me what's going on."

Carol sighed "Ok, I'll give you a time and you come talk to her at the end of your day."

"Just let me know. Does Annika do any activities during the day?"

"Ah, no, sometimes I think these people would get along better if they had some kind of job or hobby to do."

Paul had an idea… "Hey I have an idea I'll run it by my brother but have you guys ever thought of getting a garden or a vertical garden or something outside to get the patients chance to work in the open air?"

"Well, you know they did get their time outside but working in a garden or are doing something constructive that might help regulate emotions. But I know that would be hard to do especially if some of them are dangerous being around any kind of weapons."

"Well, we could only you know allow the ones that are capable of light work to do the work but it might reinforce some good psychological skills. As for Annika, it's hard to tell, I could ask king to Lisa for help because I don't think she belongs here."

"I agree, said Carol. I would hate to see her actually go crazy from being around crazy people but it might be too late."

"Let's hope not Carol for Annika's sake."

Paul was concerned. The responsibility weighed heavily on him that maybe he pushed Annika over the brink. He was determined to speak to her and find out what was bothering her. Maybe she let me read her journal, he thought anxiously. I wonder if she's said anything about me, that thought disturbed him at the prospect of having his brother read the lurid sexual encounters he and Annika had together.

Did he love her? That thought began to creep in, but he pushed it aside.

## 7

"Hey? Where are you? I have dinner ready." Lisa sent her text after Mark failed to make it home to dinner at 5.

"I'm at the office, doing some research. I'll be home in a few and I would like to talk to you about it."

"Okay, babe. What is it about?"

"Annika. She is getting worse. Carol told me she's been triggered by some strange news from Central America, and I am trying to find out what it is and why it's upsetting her. I am going to talk to her tomorrow. I'm afraid of a total breakdown."

"Okay. See you soon."

After dinner, Lisa found herself sitting in Mark's lap as he discussed his work. The topic wandered to Annika and her recent upset at the hospital.

"Carol, told me that Annika growing more obsessed with news on the Honduras coup that ousted President Zeyala and superimposed Roberto Michelleti as interim president a couple of years back." He reached for his briefcase and pulled a few papers. "Then it struck me that Annika has a slight accent. Maybe she is from Honduras or some kind of Central or South American country."

"You don't think she had something to do with that do you."

"I don't know that would be troubling if she were."

People have committed people to mental institutions to hide the truth many have tried to erase memories a lot of medical issues does seem to mirror that of those who have manipulated her memory of certain events.

"You don't think Annika is a terrorist, do you?"

"She doesn't appear to be violent."

"Looks can be deceiving though, Lisa"

"True, but I still don't feel that she is. I can start meeting with her to 3 times a week not try to help her build her memories and maybe even put her on a track to being released from here" She sat up and grabbed her laptop and googled the coup to find a short Wikipedia article on the subject. She read aloud:

"The **2009 Honduran coup d'état**, part of the **2009 Honduran constitutional crisis**,[1][2] occurred when the **Honduran Army** on June 28, 2009 followed orders from the **Honduran Supreme Court** to oust President **Manuel Zelaya** and sent him into exile.[3] The crisis was prompted when Zelaya attempted to schedule a non-binding poll on holding a **referendum** on the subject of convening a **constituent assembly** to rewrite the **constitution**.[4][5] After Zelaya refused to comply with court orders to cease, the Honduran Supreme Court secretly issued a warrant for his arrest on 26 June.[6] Two days later, Honduran soldiers stormed the president's house in the middle of the night and detained him,[7] forestalling the poll.[8] Instead of bringing him to trial, the army put him on a military aeroplane, which flew him to **Costa Rica**. Later that day, after the reading of a resignation letter of disputed authenticity, the **Honduran Congress** voted to remove Zelaya from office,[9] and appointed Speaker of Congress **Roberto Micheletti**, his constitutional successor, to replace him.[10]

**International reaction to the 2009 Honduran coup d'état** was widespread condemnation: The United Nations, the **Organization of American States** (OAS), and the **European Union** condemned the removal of Zelaya as a military coup. On 5 July 2009, all member states of the OAS voted by acclamation to suspend Honduras from the organisation."

In July 2011, Honduras's Truth Commission concluded that Zelaya had broken the law when he disregarded the Supreme Court ordering him to cancel the referendum, but that his removal from office was illegal and a coup. The Commission found Congress' designation of Roberto Micheletti as interim president as unconstitutional, and his administration as a "de facto regime." (Wikipedia.com)

Mark listened to Lisa as she read. "Those Latin American countries are rather brutal in their dealings with politics and their people."

"They have always struggled with third world issues and political strife."

Lisa continued to search the internet, "There's not much else on the subject. Looks like it's being downplayed."

Mark shifted her from one leg to another to look at her laptop. "If she's a political refugee, then I am pretty sure we won't find any documentation on her."

"Why is she here, not down there? She had to be here for a reason like an employee of the embassy here in America, maybe an interpreter perhaps?"

"I don't know, it bothers me though. She was never a drug addict or alcoholic. And she was sent here, a research institution for older people and degenerative diseases and mental issues. Whoever was in charge of getting rid of her really didn't know what they were doing,"

"Could have been Honduran authorities here in America. Could she have been a spy for the President, not sure. Most of these people get executed."

Mark sat Lisa in the chair and stood up. "Then that means they might need her again or someone wants her alive. She could have been a spy, interpreter, mistress, or all three. You'll need to talk to her and help piece things together.

"Carol said she's gotten close to Paul, maybe we should stick him with her."

Mark frowned. "Paul is finally getting back on track himself, I don't want him to fall off the wagon and say she and Paul make a serious attachment? That could be a disaster for both of them."

Lisa stood up next to him. "Let's go to bed, your mother has the kids and we need some together time."

They embraced and mutually relaxed from the weight of the situation. "I agree." He picked Lisa up and threw her over his shoulder. "Yes, you need to please your caveman husband."

"So it's role play tonight?"

"If we can squeeze it in. We have mutual ADD in our sex life and we can't do it right."

Lisa laughed all the way upstairs. "I laugh cause it's so true."

8

Paul received a text from Carol:

"Come in tomorrow at the 3:30pm. They will be in the activity room and you'll see her skipping between news channels. She may be antsy or she may not be. But that would be the best time."

He sent the usual, "okay, thanks" without getting into detail what he'd say to her. Nerves began to creep up in his soul. All he could see was her eyes the entire night keeping him awake.

Paul saw her on the couch in the big room the moment he went through the crash doors. She was in her pajamas with the remote just clicking channel after channel. She kept her eyes averted as he came to her slowly and sat down next to her.

"How are you?"

No answer. Annika kept clicking the remote.

Paul reached to remove the remote from her hand. "No, 'you ruined my life, broke my heart' slap?"

Annika started speaking fast Spanish and looked away from him. She had never spoke another language to him as long as he knew her and guilt began to grow at her melancholic face. He grabbed her shoulders and held her until she calmed down.

"You speak Spanish?"

No answer.

"Come on, give me something Annika, don't shut me out. Do you have new memories and flashbacks? Anything you remember that is disturbing you?"

She just laid in his arms breathing when the news announcer began speaking about a topic Paul knew nothing about.

"News today on the coup in Honduras. The president has been transported to Costa Rica and a new president has been selected to take over..." The news program flashed a man's face triggering a violent scream from Annika.

"Es el diablo, él es el puto diablo, que está tratando de matar a todos, he tratado de decirle a todos pero nadie me hizo caso. Vi los disparos. Vi las violaciones. Vi el asesinato, me quieren demasiado. Que alguien me ayude, alguien a salvar a los niños ..!"

She pulled herself away from Paul and fell to the floor. Carol ran to them and began to talk to her gently.

"What's wrong, Annika?" She looked up at Paul. "What did you say to her?"

Paul leaned down to put an arm around Annika. "I said nothing to her, a political story came on and she had a meltdown."

Carol looked through her bag looking for the thorazine. "Annika, I hate to have to medicate you, I'd prefer you calmed down by yourself. Paul can you tell me anything about the news program?"

He thought back. "Honduras, president removed, new president named...not much else. I don't speak Spanish so I have no clue what she said." Immense sadness began to take over.

Annika stopped crying and Paul spoke up quickly. "Carol, let me take her to her room. She'll probably get catatonic for days and God only knows for how long. I'll talk to her."

Carol helped Annika up. "Ok, take her to her room. Be careful with anything. Call for help if anything happens."

Paul put his arm over her shoulder and began to lead her to her room. They made it to the vicinity of the supply closet when his phone rang.

"Ah, Carol, I'm just about there..."

"Carol? Who's Carol?" Britney tittered.

'Ohhhhh GOD why NOW' He thought. "Look, Britney, this isn't a good time right now." His eyes grew large and he turned to see Annika glaring at him with wild eyes.

"Usted tiene una nueva mujer? ¿Qué demonios haces aquí conmigo. ¿Usted ha perdido por completo su mente. ¿Cree que puede jugar conmigo …" Annika grabbed his phone and pushed him into the unlocked supply closet. She threw it on the floor and slammed him against a wall. She fell to her knees and began to unbutton his pants and belt. Seconds later he felt her hot mouth on his body.

"Oh, fuck." He was helpless to push her off. He never noticed that Britney was still on the phone and hearing his and Annika's moans and bodies colliding.

"YOU SICK PERVE, ARE YOU FUCKING CAROL WHILE YOU ARE TALKING TO ME? WE'RE DONE. GO FIND ANOTHER HO TO SCREW." Britney cut her phone off but he was oblivious to any other person as his body released into Annika's mouth. He panted heavily adrenaline raged through his body. He fell to his knees in front of her and put an arm around her. Tears began to stream down his face.

Annika put her head on his shoulder. He grabbed her face and kissed her sweetly.

"I am so sorry for hurting you. This is all my fault." He sat down exhausted.

Annika grabbed his arm. "We should go. I've been so lonely without you. I can't hold to my sanity anymore. I'm scared." She had tears in her eyes.

He got her and they stood up. He pulled up his pants and adjusted her shirt.

"Come on. You need a nap."

He sat with her in her room for 15 minutes until she slept peacefully. He wiped his face and evidence of other activities they had done and as he walked out of her room, was stopped by Lisa.

"Paul, what are you doing here? And coming out of Annika's room?"

"I, ah, I was here to see Carol, and Annika had a slight meltdown. Carol asked me to bring her to her room.

"Melt down?"

"Ah, yes, she was watching the news and something about the Honduras came on, and she lost it, rattled off in Spanish, and just fell to the ground."

Lisa had a stern look. "I know you used to work here, but Carol shouldn't have let you take her to her room in the state she was in. She should have sent for 2 scrub orderlies to take her to her room. Annika could have become violent and have hurt you seriously. Did she try anything with you, Paul?"

"Ah, no, she was tired after being really active so we made it to her room and she's taking a nap now."

"Oh, she's asleep?"

"Yes, for the moment."

Lisa opened her door and peeked in.

"I see. Well, I am glad it was nothing. Come over to the house and see us some time, we miss you. Your mother said you had a new place now."

"Yes. And speaking of said apartment, I need to speak to the landlord about some issues with plumbing." He grinned. Get it together, Paul, his brain screamed.

Lisa smiled. "Just come and visit. Joel has his crazy fantasy football nonsense to blather and bore you with." She walked with him to the front office.

She watched him walk out the doors towards the parking lot.

"Is Paul and Carol seeing each other? That could get messy. Eesh, Paul." She muttered.

Carol was also worried when Paul showed back up at 1:13 am.

"Paul, what are you doing here?"

"I left my phone here and I promised that I'd see Annika I'd come see her." He lied. He just had to see her. "Plus, I do need to make updates to the system." Thank God for the truth, He muttered. "I'll set up the updates and wait for them to upload while watching a movie with Annika."

Carol wasn't buying it. "Paul, everyone thinks you and I are having a fling but I think it's you and Annika." She grabbed his arm. "Are you in love with her?" He pulled away and walked to the office computer.

Carol grabbed him again. "Look, Annika is not a girlfriend, she has problems she needs to deal with. If you are here to take advantage of her, not only could you get into trouble but we could lose Annika forever. "

She dropped his arm and reached in her purse. "The janitor found this in the supply closet today and there was a smear stain on the floor that resembled semen. Now I'll cover for you but if this comes in between me and my husband or job, you're busted."

Paul took his phone and noticed the crack where Annika had slung it to the wall. He put it in his work bag and headed out to the hall towards her room.

"Carol."

She looked up at him looking back at her.

"I do love her."

Carol sighed loud and watched him slip into Annika's room.

Annika bounced up from her bed and ran to him. "Paul, what are you doing here?"

He turned to her. "I had to see you."

She grabbed him and kissed him deeply until he pushed her off. "Hey, we are going to take a break from sex for a while."

"Well, what are we going to do?"

Paul grinned. "I brought a movie and my laptop. The whole Fast and Furious series."

Annika grabbed the dvds. "Fast and Furious?"

"Oh it's these thieves that drive supped up fast cars and steal but turn good and drive fast cars in other parts of the world....You'll like it..." he looked at her with a small grin. "Are you wearing Tweety Bird pajamas?"

She looked up with a silly look on her face. 'Well, yes, I love Tweety Bird."

He pulled her to him and kissed her. "Let's start that whole not doing it thing tomorrow."

Thirty minutes later, they were both lying in her bed watching the 1$^{st}$ movie.

"You see, Paul Walker's character is trying to bust Vin Diesel's character for stealing property by hijacking truck drivers, however, they become good friends and eventually Paul Walker's character lets him go in this movie, but asks Vin Diesel's character to join the FBI in later movies to bust real bad guys."

"That makes no sense."

Paul laughed. "Nah, you're right, but guys love fast cars and racing and that's basically the movie. Racing and pulling crazy stunts."

"Oh, you men will do anything to get yourselves killed." She sat up and grabbed the other dvd case. "So this is the same movie in every sequel?"

Paul wiped the tears from his eye from laughing. "Yes...I thought you'd love all the Spanish parts."

"You're a dork. Seriously".

"Oh, I know, but your face is making me laugh harder than anything else, right now."

Annika rolled her eyes and sat up. She grabbed a blanket and wrapped it around her shoulders to stare in the early morning moonlight. Paul got up to stand with her and held her from behind.

"Things are starting to come back for me." She whispered.

"What things?"

"People talking. Much madness. Being taken. White flashes in my head and big empty spots of things in the middle of memories."

"I hear words and parts of words. There are men talking of taking people away, transporting drugs and guns. People also talk of crazy men talking about making us smaller by killing people. Some talk of stealing children. Then it goes black and I have to wait for more from my brain."

"It sounds like your brain is healing. Did you hit your head or did someone hit you hard?"

"I don't know.  I can't remember."

He held her tighter. "It'll come back. We really do need to give the sex fun a rest for a while and you tell Lisa everything that's happening."

Carol walked in without invitation. "Time to go, Paul. I can't let you stay in here all night. She needs sleep and you don't want jail, do you?

"Just five more minutes, Carol!"

"Okay. Just say your goodbyes and meet me out in the hall.

"Hey" He looked into Annika's eyes. "I'm always going to be around. You just focus on getting better and getting out of here and I'll steal you away from the world."

She smiled. "Oh you are so silly and dramatic."

"No, I'm serious. I'm serious this time. For the first time ever." He kissed her long and softly. He gathered his stuff and headed for her door. "I'll be back, I promise."

Carol held the door for him. 'You know, you really do tend to be reckless in your actions, Paul."

"I sometimes screw things up, yes."

"Well, this time you better not. Now you have me involved in your little sexscapade with a patient. I have a lot more to lose than you."

Paul walked into the office and checked the update. "I'm going to have to check the hall videos and delete you from them." She countered.

Paul stood back up and walked to the door where she stood. He planted a kiss on her forehead. "Don't worry, Carol, I have this under control. And thanks for the help, lover."

She slapped his arm. "Yep, this will blow up in our faces."

He laughed and left the hospital in a cheerful mood.

"He what?" Mark choked on his coffee the next morning.

'He's supposedly having a relationship with Carol."

"But Carol's married....happily married," Mark sputtered.

"I know. But they say noises were coming out of the supply closet and then they found Paul's phone on the floor. I called the last person, who by the way, is bat shit Britney, and she said...and I quote, 'They were making moans and body sounds that would put a porno to shame. I'm tired of Paul's sucky lame ass and it's over for good.' End quote."

Mark gagged.

"Mark? What's wrong?"

"I, ah, I just had a visual on Paul and Carol..."

"In the closet?"

Mark gagged again. Joel laughed. "Uncle Paul is tapping that ass."

Lisa and Mark looked at Joel with the stink eye. "Don't talk like that at the table. Hush your mouth," Lisa admonished.

"But MOM!"

"You are 13 years old, I better not hear of "tapping ass" either."

Mark gagged and ran to the sink. "How in the hell can Paul make an even worse decision than what he normally does."

Joel chuckled. "Paul can have a girlfriend if he wants, what's the big deal?"

Lisa evil-eyed Joel, "You're pushing it, Joel. You know Carol is married and has kids. You shouldn't be dating someone who is married."

Mark threw his coffee cup against the wall and they all watched it break into a thousand pieces.

"MARK!" Lisa looked at the children. "Kids, go get your book bags and eat your breakfast in the living room."

The kids got up mumbling. Joel muttered "I still don't know what's the big deal." As he passed his mother and she grabbed his arm. "Boy, one more word out of you and I pack up your PS3 for good and you wash all the toilets and the dog house."

"Okay, okay, I'm just in a good mood, don't punish me for that!"

Lisa let him walk on out.

Mark shook his head. "See, we've got our own Paul now," He sat back down. "I'll toss him out on his ass if he causes problems. I can't lose Carol, she's kept that place together for the last 12 years."

Lisa smiled ruefully and sat back next to him. "This is all coming from community college Barbie and we all know she's got her hands and face all up in crack. This could all be a rumor to get back at Paul. But really, I don't think Carol is the type and Paul would lose his lunch if Marty her husband came after him."

"You know, Paul should have 6 six foot 5 construction black man charge up in that hospital and make Paul shit his pants. He needs to shit his pants once or twice in his life."

Lisa laughed. "Oh get it together, Mark. Remember you are Paul's brother and not his father. AND you are no stranger to having issues. Just because you overcame them, doesn't make you better."

"Lisa, his scrawny, over-sexed cassanova ass is going to drive me to DRINKING!"

"And obviously cursing."

Mark stopped the tirade and stared at his plate.

"You're right. But I am going to have a chat with him."

Lisa went to the sink to wash dishes. "Now, Mark, don't say anything you'll..."

She heard Mark slam the door.

"...regret."

## 9

Paul humming a tune under his breath found his morning a bit troublesome as he opened his office door and turned the light on.

"Hello there, sexy."

His brother swiveled around in his chair to look at him.

"Oh, Mark, how's it going?

"Oh, it goes well. I was just checking to see if you had condoms available for, you know, any available piece of ass."

Paul looked at him. "What are you talking about?

"Um, someone has shared with me, lover boy, that you and Carol are doing the big nasty. I hope I described that right?"

Paul couldn't help but laugh. "Well, I tried with her but she shut me down."

"Oh did she now?"

"Yes."

"You know fraternizing with other employees on the clock can get you fired, right, PAULUS?"

He was laughing even harder. "Carol and I aren't doing it."

"The janitor found your phone in the supply closet. Lisa called the last number and Britney answered and said you were "banging the shit" out of Carol."

"Britney? You mean you believe drug addict weed-brain Britney over me? She and I haven't seen each other in 6 months. Carol was probably helping me get rid of her."

"I know! Let's call Carol and ask!"

Paul's smile fell. "Why?"

"Just to make sure this rumor is a figment of a rehab reject."

Mark took out his phone and dialed Carol's home phone and put it on speaker phone.

"Hello?"

"Yes, Carol, this is Mark? Me and Paul are here to talk about the rumors about you and he in the closet."

"Oh.....the closet."

Paul leaned in and explained the moment to Carol, hoping she's get what he was saying. "Hey, Carol, Mark was here telling me about my phone in the closet and how people were thinking that you and I were having an affair or some such crap."

Carol's nervous laugh came through the phone. "Yes! That's completely false, I've answered his phone at times trying to help him to get rid of her so sometimes I pretended to be his new girl. But no. Just a rumor."

Mark sounded relieved. "Well, Carol, you would never lie to me so I believe you. I was just making sure that if HR contacted me, I would know the whole story."

Paul grinned. "Yes, Mark is just getting sensitive to drama in his old age."

Mark looked up him sternly. "Ok Carol. I am glad you straightened that up for me. We can't afford any issues at this research hospital and I know you wouldn't do anything to destroy this hospital or anything."

Paul muttered. "Destroy, sheesh...Ok, Godfather."

Carol laughed again. "Dr. Mark, you know I love it there."

"Yes, I do. You take care and see you soon."

"See? Paul relaxed "You were overreacting....again." He covered his face with his hands.

Mark got up and walked a towards the office door.

"Next time, Mark, could you just call a person before you get all high-handed with your psychological sleuthing." He got up and started for his desk.

Mark grabbed him and pushed against the wall.

"I don't think you grasp the importance of what we do here. We have elderly patients that we help get a few shreds of their memory back to remember their grandchildren. We have elderly vets living here for free because they'd be on the street with no family to care for them. We also work to educate others that come for day treatment that helps them live on their own without being committed against their will. I have responsibility over these people and I am not letting a middle 30's playboy come in and wreck their lives if we get desolved." He let Paul go and straightened his shirt.

Paul stepped away. "You have become a Dr. Phil godfather. Your vein is popping."

"Look, Paul. I know you want to find some stability among other things, but let me remind you of one thing, no good girl is going to be with an unstable man who can't keep his pants on and can't stay focused longer than the last bender. Now I see you are making progress, but you need to make you sure know that you work here, some of my responsibility is now your responsibility. For better or for worse, we're now in this together. These people rely on you as much as they do me. Just keep that in mind when you are acting impulsively or just thinking of your own needs. I think you grown a heart to help these people if I'm not mistaken. Do please remember that, okay?"

Paul stood looking at the floor silently.

"I still love you, Paulus, and I think you are getting better." He walked out the door.

"Love you too, Markie." He whispered.

"Oh, I could kick you for all this drama, Paul!"

Carol spoke out loud as the only other person in the break room walked out of their leaving them alone.

"I'm really sorry, Carol, I never meant to get you dragged into any of this."

"I checked on Annika, she is doing much better. You are a good influence on her."

Paul stood awkwardly. "She's a great girl. I really don't think she belongs here."

"I agree." Carol leaned in closer. "Have you ever heard of electroshock therapy?"

"What?"

"Yes. I've been reading up on it and Annika seems to show signs of recovering from electroshock therapy."

Realization descended into his brain about what Annika had been tortured to keep quiet. Rage began to boil up in his soul.

"No. Not electroshock therapy."

"Yes, I'm afraid so."

"How does someone recover from that?"

"Depended on how healthy they are some never do I hate to say it but these episodes are a good sign that she is actually healing."

"Is there anything that I can do?"

"And the best thing you can do is just to be really good friends with her allowed her to talk to you but not put it into a sexual relationship."

"That I can do. I already told her that we can't be together that way anymore."

"How you managed to get out of being caught for this is unbelievable. The best thing to do now is to drop it for the both of you. That's not to say that one day you and she will never be together I just don't think this is a good time for either one of you."

Paul grew silent. He knew she was telling the truth.

"It's going to be really hard. I do love her."

"Tell me what happened in the supply closet."

"I was trying to take her back to her room and she pushed me in there and she performed a sex act on me. She lost it when she heard me talking to Brittany on the phone.

"So technically she assaulted you"

"Well if you want to call it that."

Carol sighed. "I don't think she knew what she was doing. Did she have a blank look on her face?"

"Yes."

"Then yes, she didn't know what she was doing.  She had a lack of impulse control and emotional restraint. Paul, you and she having sex was really a bad thing but somehow you triggered something in her brain to remember."

"I have the penis that heals." He quipped

Carol rolled her eyes. "Well, let's restrain the healing penis for a bit, shall we?"

Paul laughed. "You are very good at this, why haven't you gone to school to be a psychologist yourself?"

Carol laughed. "I'll look into it. I'll keep your secret, but don't make me regret it."

Paul kissed her cheek. "You may be in danger of being stolen from Marty. We could all move to a place where polygamy is accepted."

"Smart ass. Marty's got it where it counts. I could never walk away from him. We're childhood sweethearts."

"I have some ideas for Mark that can keep me around here to keep and eye on Annika. I promise no more lurid events of drama."

"I'm holding you to it Paul."

They left the break room separately so no one would think anything. 'Gotta keep ahead of the gossipers', he thought. 'But I do have an idea on being close to Annika without anyone noticing.' He laughed deviously.


It had only taken a day for Paul to get all his ideas together. He thought that researching gardening and exercise therapy for elderly people would be a great idea to have at the hospital. The patients did get outside time in a secluded area but it wasn't a spacious lot where people could grow a vegetable garden or a small garden of flowers to relax and take their minds away from their worries. He thought it would make a great research are for Mark and Lisa to use there at the hospital and he could come after work to help take care of its basic needs. "In which could go deep into the weekend nights." Paul said to himself, smiling. "That would give me so much time with her to get to know her a little better and find out more about her past."

He knew Lisa would love it. He knew Mark would ask how they would pay for it. So he even stopped by their accountant's office so that he could have him fit into the research budget.

"So, here are the benefits of creating a working vertical garden for the health and strength of the elderly in coping with their mental and physical disabilities. I found this article online, **https://www.betterhealth.vic.gov.au/health/healthyliving/gardening-for-older-people**, says,

**"Benefits of gardening for older people"**

Gardening is beneficial for older people because it:

- Is an enjoyable form of exercise
- Increases levels of physical activity and helps mobility and flexibility
- Encourages use of all motor skills
- Improves endurance and strength
- Helps prevent diseases like osteoporosis
- Reduces stress levels and promotes relaxation
- Provides stimulation and interest in nature and the outdoors
- Improves wellbeing as a result of social interaction
- Can provide nutritious, home-grown produce.

I think this is something worth researching to find out if there are better ways of treating the elderly."

Mark looked at him with half disbelief and half interest. "Why are you so interested in doing this with my patients?"

Paul shifted a bit. "Well, I go to know them rather well, and I miss spending time with them. I can help manage and do the hard labor and oversee the work after my day shift is over. I could spend a couple of hours during the week and use the weekends to help with upkeep. Hey, maybe you can get Annika to help me too." He slid that last part in innocently.

Mark gave him a side look. "Annika appears to be struggling with flashbacks and repressed memories coming back to the surface. Lisa, Carol, and I are concerned that she could lash out at people until she can get them resolved."

"Carol told me about it. I think getting out of her room and the television is a good idea. She was getting obsessed with the news. "

"You might be right. These are good ideas, I promise I'll take a look at them and talk to Lisa about it. I'll just tell you, she'll think it's a great idea. If we can't do it here at the hospital, we can ask a farmer to donate some land or we might even rent or buy it. This is something legitimate. Anything else you think you need?

"How bout a tv and entertainment system for my office?"

"Uh no."

"I just thought I'd try. So Lisa doesn't hate me?"

"Lisa never hated you. No, Mom and Lisa think you walk on water even though you've been teaching our son idiomatic sex slurs."

"Oh, he could get those at school too."

Mark rolled his eyes. "He got it from his uncle and those Saturday morning Call of Duty games."

"Oh yes, tell Joel that Matt24 said he wanted to join our special forces crew."

"Paul, seriously, you're 34 almost 35."

"So, many grown men still play video games. Well, if it makes you happy, if you sign off on this, I won't be playing Call of Duty as much with Joel."

"You just sold me on it."

"Oh, I can tell how much you love me."

"I can't tell you how much I am happy to see our metrosexual blonde tips gone and our regular brown hair back."

"Forgive me if I refuse to settle in for the Clark Gable greased look yet."

"Ok, Ok, OK, Enough, I am just messing with you, don't go out of here all butt hurt."

"Did you just say butt hurt?" Paul shook his head. "Yeah, I have to go. Dinner tonight you said?"

"Yep, bring the cannolis." He said in his best Godfather accent.

"The sad thing here is that you really find yourself funny. I'll see ya." Paul rolled his eyes, turned, and walked out of his office.

"So, here's what we plan to do here." Dr. Flint said in an employee meeting. "Paul has shown us a new research plan to test mental and physical activity at the hospital so that maybe we can help the patients better."

"We are going to either purchase land or use a small plot her on the grounds and have patients being led by our own Paul to maintain the plants and the gardening. I'll need the orderlies and the nurses to write down data on data sheets that we are going to proved to track any interesting changes that occur in the patients, upswings in memory, behaviors, cognitive gains from this. And if this does show a suitable course of therapy, then Lisa and I will present the findings to the Academy of psychological clinical science for review and publishing.

Lisa spoke up." This could actually lead to more research money and maybe we can build our own facility not too far away but eventually be independent from the main hospital. That means helping more people and being a good alternative to other state run facilities that just lock crazy people until they die."

"Yes, Lisa is right. We can all do some good here. And of course, with new money come raises that all of you deserve. So this is on the agenda for the next 6 months. IF you have any questions, you'll have to ask Paul. He'll be the one in charge of this project." Mark looked at Paul. "He's the brain behind this scheme."

Paul blushed red and nodded his head. It was the first time his brother ever gave him any credit for good work. He almost had to walk out and was a bit more fidgety in the rest of the meeting. 'I hope I can see Annika today.' He pulled out a pic on his phone he had of her and stared at it not hearing when Mark and Lisa ended the meeting.

"Come on, get up." He heard Carol say.

He got up and followed Carol blindly not really thinking about where they were going until he found himself in an outside secluded waiting area and looked up to see Annika's bright smiling face looking at him. He grabbed her and held her close.

"You are a sight for sore eyes."

He looked down in her face. "You seem happier.

"Yes. I have been getting therapy and treatment and Dr. Flint prescribed me medicine that helps keep the emotions less potent so I can sort through my thoughts trying to come back. I've been so perky that all the angry old people hate me now."

They walked in the waiting area and sat down on a bench and listen to the cheap water fountain bubbling.

"I'm going to be around here more. I have a project that I am in charge of and I'll get to see you more."

She beamed. "That sounds great."

"AND, I asked that you be allowed to help me with it, so now you are technically my employee now."

She laughed. "So we should be keep behaving? I talked to Lisa and I am getting more stable so they are thinking about putting me in a controlled apartment around here so I can get some freedom back."

"So, we might have our own little love shack soon?" He pulled her head close and kissed her lightly on the lips.

She laughed. "Yes."

Carol cleared her throat. "Ok, lovebirds.....time to go. You'll see each other soon enough."

They stood up and walked back to the door where Carol stood. "Hey, keep a look out, wouldja?" Paul said.

He grabbed Annika's face and gave her a long deep kiss.

"Stay safe." He whispered.

"I will."

Carol rolled her eyes. "Oh you two are breaking my heart."

"Carol, doesn't Marty still romance you?" Paul quipped as he had his arm around Annika's neck.

Carol laughed. "I'm married, those days are over. We just have 30-40 minutes of nasty sex before Jimmy Fallon every Tuesday, Thursday, and weekends."

Paul made a face. "You have a sex schedule?"

Carol snorted. "You guys make it to 20 years, you will too, now let's go, Annika." She grabbed her arm and led her back to her room. Annika turned around and waved back with a smile. Paul walked away down the other hall with a permanent smile for the rest of the day.

## 10

Spring arrived and they had managed to have a local farm to give them a place to build a working garden. The farming family had horses and Paul had asked permission to ride a few for pleasure. Spurred on by a moment of impulse, he rode up on Annika and Carol in the vineyard hanging grape plants. He pulled the mare to a stop.

"Hey, Carol, I need to borrow Annika, we need to go scope out some more property." Before she could argue, he reached out an arm to Annika and jumped on the horse's back in front of them. He kicked the horse to move and he and Annika took off to the far end of the pasture. They got off the mare and let her graze while he took her to a small brook to sit and talk.

"I found this place and I knew that if I had the chance to bring you, I would."

Annika smiled. "I like it, it's very pretty." She walked around the little wooded area looking for a place to sit. She chose an indentation in the ground by a large maple tree. Paul slyly slid right next to her and pulled her close.

"What's a hot girl like you doing in a place like this?" His voice drawled like syrup.

"I'm at the mercy of an evil fiend looking to steal my virtue."

"Oh, you mean me, my lady."

"Yes, you are very devastating."

Annika blushed. They locked eyes for a moment.

He rushed in and kissed her full on the mouth and then laid her on her back on the ground. His hands moved up her t-shirt and squeezed her breast. She let out a pleasure sigh. He felt her hands reach in between his pants about to snap them open.

"ANNIKA?"

Mark's voice slashed through the sound of the forest.

"Oh SHIT." He breathed and dropped her completely.

Both didn't breathe for 10 seconds until they heard Mark's booming voice come closer towards them to the stream. "Ok, tell them that you wandered off, and I came looking for you."

"Why was I the one that was lost? Why can't that be you, and I found you."

"Cause I said so." Before she could complain more, he jumped up and yelled back

"Hey, Mark, you were looking for Annika too? Hey, I found her right here by the river." He helped her stand up and they started walking to Mark.

"Annika, you can't be walking around by yourself in the woods." Mark's fatherly voice was gentle trying to explain to her the dangers of the woods, animals, and people that could harm her. He grabbed her upper arm and led her away. She flashed a mean look back at Paul. He shrugged as he got back on the horse and rode up to them.

"You are so right, Mark, you need to drill it into her head that blind daydreaming is very dangerous and not paying attention is very important." He laughed as he rode off to the house with Annika shooting daggers at his back with her eyes.

Annika sat in her room late at night writing in her journal when Paul walked in to see her.

"Hey."

She stood up and said hey, before he closed her lips with his. Their tongues played together for what felt like minutes until she started swaying from weak knees. He put an arm around her waist.

"You still wet from earlier? Let me check." He slid his fingers in her pajamas and rubbed her clit insistently, she covered his fingers in her wetness.

"Oh you still are. We shouldn't let that go to waste." He pulled his fingers out and pushed them between her lips. She played with his fingertips with her tongue.

He turned her away from him and began to undress her. When done, he began to remove his clothes. He sat down in her chair and pulled her on his lap on top of his hardness. He started moving her against him until they shared her wet cum. He softly pushed himself in her and whispered "Love me, babe."

She began to move up and down, up and down and began to increase her speed while he pulled her back to his chest and grabbing her breast hard. Quickly he stood up and threw her on her bed, pushing her back down, head shoved into the mattress and took her hard from behind, not stopping until he'd lost his orgasm hard.

Their breathing finally eased down after 10 minutes. He laid face down beside her with an arm over her back.

They laid there in the moonlight on her bed.

"Paul."

"Mm."

"Where do we go from here?"

"If I had my choice, it would be to Five Guys for a double cheeseburger."

She popped his chest.

"No, I mean future. Do you see us together or is this something that will fade away the longer it goes?"

He sat up and looked into her eyes. "I don't know, Annika. Much of us being together means we have to keep quiet about this, and you have to get better and, we have to get you out of this place as a patient."

"Well, I have been seeing Lisa, and she says I can start a new exiting program and live off the hospital with outpatient care. She's offered to be my therapist to sign off and make sure I can handle the pressures of living on my own, but she's seen enough progress from me to give it a 6 month trial."

Paul's eyes lit. "That's great! Now we can do things together outside of this mad house."

"But what would Mark say?"

"He'd be mad as hell."

"He wouldn't try to stop us, would he?"

"He might."

"He…he can't..." She grabbed his face. "I love you too much."

He stared in her eyes for a long weighty moment. He pulled her to him. "I won't let him."

She held onto him for a long while until she slept deeply. He eased her on her bed, turned off her light, and then slipped out the door. He had some work to do if he wanted them to be together and he had to get ahead of Mark before he figured anything out.

## 11

Lisa sat quietly while she waited for Annika to respond. She and Annika were trying suggestive hypnosis to find the reason behind bright flashes with broken memories that would cause a dull headache every time they occurred,

"I see files."

"What's going on with the files?"

"Being shredded, then burned."

"Can you read them?"

"Yes, in Spanish."

"What does it say?"

"We plan to take the president to another country, and then..." She stopped.

"Then what."

"A male voice. He yells at me and everything goes blank." She grabbed her head. "The lights are flashing again and I have a tingling pain everywhere in my body. Nothing."

Lisa wrote this down on her notepad. Every memory ends this way. 'Someone tried to erase her mind' she mused.

"Annika, do you feel the pain in the evening?"

"No, it goes away before dinner."

"Hm. I would expect it to act like a multi day migraine but the headaches are short now. What do you do in the evening?"

"Well, I help Paul with the patients with his little gardening plans."

"I see, so the interaction and the fresh air probably release the necessary endorphins to counteract the pain. Not sure that gardening is that intense of an activity to release the amount needed to completely heal the pain. Is there anything else that you do?

She flashed a confused face. "Uh not that I am aware."

"Do you masturbate?"

Annika grew beet red and shook her head profusely.

"You should, it could help with relieving stress and anxiety."

Annika sat there mildly shocked at Lisa's words.

"Do you masturbate?" Annika couldn't help but ask.

Lisa shrugged not missing a beat. "Not very often because Dr. Flint and I have a healthy sex life. Mark is quite a learned lover."

"What about Paul?"

Lisa looked up at her. "I wouldn't know about Paul. I know he's made poor choices in the past with girlfriends, but I can see him being amorous like his brother."

Annika felt lost at this conversation. She wanted to tell Lisa about making love to Paul and how much she loved him. She knew though that they would separate them. She hesitated to share the details about their love at least without telling Paul first.

Lisa continued. "The day will come when you will seek a physical relationship with a man again and I encourage you to be open to intimacy. It can further help unlock these chains holding you back from living. I also secured an apartment close to the hospital and we've covered the cost all utilities and furniture. I also have a job with the hospital and you are now on payroll as an assistant. As Carol tells me, doing what you already do to help her. Don't be afraid to live life now. We will keep these meetings up and continue to monitor your situation." She looked at her med list. "Why are you on birth control?"

"Uh, I don't know."

"I'm taking you off for the time being. You need your normal hormones for total recuperation and since you are not sexually active, I don't see a problem taking you off that medication."

"Yes, ma'am."

"If you have any urges or sexual feelings that come up or make you feel awkward, let me know and we'll work through them in therapy, ok?"

"Yes, ma'am."

"You can call me Lisa if you want."

"Uh, yes ....Lisa."

"Good. I'll see you next week."

Paul was on Annika's room floor that night laughing crazily with what Lisa said to her that day in therapy.

"So my sweet sister n-law suggested masturbation? She didn't offer to show a few moves?" He wiped tears from his eyes. "Oh, that was good. I needed that."

"I fail to see how this so funny."

Paul sat back on her bed beside her. "Cause you are getting real sex not masturbation but we can start doing that instead of sex if you want." He raised an eyebrow and leaned in to kiss her.

She held back a second. "Hey, what's this about birth control? I never asked for birth control."

"Oh, I suggested that Mark prescribe that to you when we started having our blatant illicit affair many many months ago."

"Well, Lisa has taken it off."

"What!"

"Yes."

Paul's face jumbled in irritation. "Dammit. This means we have to use condoms and other means to make sure you don't get pregnant."

"This might not be a problem when I move out a few weeks from now on my own."

Paul looked sad. "I'll be sad that we can't see each other only here as employees. Maybe we should use the supply closet again and masturbate." He smiled cheekily at her.

"Oh yes, that would be a brilliant idea, Paul."

Paul sprawled on the bed and pulled her beside him. They stared at the ceiling and talked quietly.

"Maybe I could move in with you."

"Dr. Flint will allow that?"

"Nah, you're right." He paused. "Unless...."

"Unless what?"

"We get married."

Annika sat up. "You can't be serious."

"Thanks, I love you too. Thanks for giving me hope you'll say yes."

"Oh stop, of course, I'd say yes. But do you think this is something we should do?"

"I don't see why not. We are adults in our late thirties. If we do it secretly, then Mark can't stop us."

Annika looked worried. "I don't know, Paul, I feel like there is something out there dark and menacing that is waiting to destroy us."

"Oh, you are just being silly, I'd never let anyone hurt you."

"It's not that...I could have been involved in something really bad. It scares me to think that could show up here and hurt people."

Paul sat up and looked into her eyes. "I will never let anyone hurt you ever. I would kill them if they tried. Don't even let any of those thoughts invade your soul. You and I will be together I can promise you that."

## 12

Paul began making plans for him and Annika. He found himself enjoying the process, planning on them being together every day just living life like normal people with no worries. He continue to slip in every other night to spend time with her but the no sex rule many times was ignored since neither one could resist each other's touch for too long.

He began to picture a house with kids running around inside with Annika walking around and presiding over the family with her mothering eyes. She was the perfect mold for a mother to him. His mind wandered to her being pregnant and then they being happy parents of a beautiful baby boy or girl. "I wonder what we would name the baby?' He pondered. He hated his lonely apartment. He volunteered to help Mark and Lisa move Annika out into her apartment and he felt morose the entire time.

He felt many times as just blurting it out to his brother. He somewhat wanted him to be a part of his plans and get his approval with his decision to marry Annika. He and Annika continued to remain quiet and avoid any type of outward showing of their affection. It proved to be hard because he now saw her every day. And every day he asked himself the same burning question, "What color are her panties today?"

She flashed him her big smile along with her doe brown eyes shining. Only Carol could see the interactions on their faces and sometimes she laughed at them until she cried. Other days, she began to show signs of concern for both of them since it had become more stressful to endure. She encouraged Paul to open up to his brother. Still he refused.

The hospital was its own little quiet world. New faces began to appear. Mark had hired a new security guard along with the nightshift orderlies and assistants. Annika had her own place and Paul was sneaking over there every other night. The clandestine meetings at the hospital were falling scarce.

One Friday, he and Annika met up on a lonely back hall.

"You holding up well?"

She had a tired smile, "Yes, been tired but I am still making it through the day."

He pulled her close and grabbed her ass and squeezed. "You should call in sick tomorrow. Then I can take the afternoon off and update your server."

She smiled. "Update my server? That's a new one."

He leaned in and kissed her deeply.


"Well, would you look at this."

Mitch, the new security guard, leaned in and watched them make out on the security camera monitor.

"She must be the local gal that gives to the big boys in charge. Yea, that's the head doctor's brother in charge of the computer systems."

His eyes glazed over as he began to move towards his pants.

"Yes, I might tap that soon." He zoomed in on Annika's face.

## 13

Carlos Montoya sat listening to steps rushing towards his office door. A private in his army stepped in and hastily announced his success at his mission.

"General, we have found five of the missing dissidents."

"Good, you know what to do."

The sergeant turned around and walked into the office and handed back out into the yard. General Montoya stood and watched as the sergeant instructed the men to blindfold the five people and place them in front of a firing squad. After several bangs, the bloody bodies laid still on the ground.

"Han ubicados cada uno en esa lista?" Have you located everyone on that list?"

""Todos menos uno." "All but one." He threw a file with it to look as if on the death of the general.

""Éste parece desaparecer. Fue un intérprete que trabajó en los Estados Unidos". "This one seems to disappear. She was an interpreter that worked in the United States."

The general opened the file and noticed that her last location was Washington, DC, 2009.

The sergeant continued. "No hemos encontrado en el paradero de la mujer pasada en Centroamérica o Estados Unidos".We haven't found in the whereabouts of the last woman in Central America or United States."

The General shook his head.   "No seguir mirando. Ella tuvo contacto personal y el acceso a todo el mundo, estoy seguro de que los americanos le esconden. "No keep looking. She had personal contact and access to everyone, I'm sure the Americans are hiding her."

" Pero ¿cómo será encontrarla?  "But how will we find her?"

 "Seguir buscando . " Just keep looking." He stood and looked outside. "Ella aparecerá.

She'll turn up." He opened up the file.

"Encuentra a esta mujer." "Find this woman." He pulled a picture of an elderly Hispanic woman. "Su madre sabría dónde fue vista por última vez." "Her mother would know where she was last seen."

The sergeant nodded and left immediately.


Annika noticed that the new security guard had begun to follow her around the hospital halls. She began to be concerned when Mitch began trying to talk to her at lunch.

"Hey, there pretty girl."  Mitch, a tall scrawny man, sauntered to her like a cowboy.  His beady eyes did not hide his lurid intentions.  Annika bristled at his high pitched southern drawl.  She could tell he wanted more than friendship.

"I'm new here. How long have you been working here?"

Annika chewed her sandwich slowly. "I just started working here a few weeks ago."

Mitch grinned. "Know anyone else here?"

"Uh, no, I don't."

Mitch leaned closer. "You sure about that?"

Annika tried to move away from him.

"Cause I think you are giving some people here some special attention."

He kept moving closer. She could smell mild body odor mixed with egg salad. She began mildly gagging.

"I saw you getting all sweet on the computer boss." He put his arm around her.

He leaned closer to her ears. "I know you ain't supposed to be giving head personnel special attention. So... if you want your secret safe with me, you'll have to share. The whispered breath tickled her ear.

"I have to get back to work." She stumbled out of her chair and walked away hurriedly. She almost ran over Carol in the hall. After ignoring her calls she headed to the restroom.

Paul walked into the head office at the next day to get a chance to see Annika and speak with his friends. He noticed that Annika had been acting weird in had not called him at all.

Carol sat thoughtfully. "Are you and Annika still together?" she whispered.

"Yes."

"She's been acting weird. She started to show signs of having a relapse. I don't know what the trigger is.

"Carol, do you think she can actually live on her own."

"Yes I think she can. I think there's just some things that we don't know about."

Paul and Carol sat and chatted lightly until Paul looked up at the computer video monitors. He saw the new security guard pulling Annika into the side closet. He had his hands all over her body and forcing her to kiss him.

Paul snapped into action and burst through the office door running to the closet. He wrenched to the door open and pulled Mitch off o Annika who had fallen to the floor. He began to punch Mitch in the face and until Carol pulled him off of him. She pressed the button on the wall for the other security guards aimed for mark to come quickly into the hospital ward. The other security guards came and handcuffed Mitch to take him away. Mark came momentarily after he heard the emergency buzzer. He helped restrain Paul as Carol looked after Annika.

"What happened here?" He boomed.

"Your new security guard was trying to rape Annika!" Paul spat out.

"Are you sure?"

"It's on the dam monitor. Go see for yourself."

Paul got on his knees and helped Carol revive Annika.

"Why are you so worked up, Paul?"

"No reason. I just hate seeing women abused."

Mark followed the security guards. In the pit of his stomach he knew something wasn't right.

"Guys, put Mitch in the conference room. I want to talk to him before the police come."

He walked in the conference room. He barely contained his anger as he began to question Mitch about Annika.

"Why did you do that to her?"

Mitch laughed. "I thought you all knew already. I thought she was giving it up to all you head honchos."

"Why would you think that?"

"Cause I saw it all on the monitor."

"Saw what on monitor."

"I saw her and your brother making out on the screen and apparently, it's very serious."

"Mitch, I don't know what you saw but hospital staff and patients are not allowed to have sexual relations."

"Watch the tapes, it's there. Your brother and that broad."

Mark started seeing flashes of light as he pulled the door open and yelled for Carol.

"CAROL! Where's Carol? Buzz Carol! Get Carol down here now!"

Carol and Paul were still a trying to rouse Annika when she was buzzed to the front office.

"Stay with her. I have to go to the head office."

She left in a hurry just as Annika started coming to.

"He wouldn't leave me alone."

"It's ok. Don't try to talk."

He sat at holding her quietly when the police walked into the closet.

"The guy you're looking for is at the head office."

"Are you Paul Flint?"

"Yes."

"Then it's you we are here for. Stand up, turn round and put your hands above your head. You have the **right** to remain silent. Anything you say can and will be used against you in a court of law. You have the **right** to speak to an attorney, and to have an attorney present during any questioning. If you cannot afford a lawyer, one will be provided for you at government expense."

"Wait, wait I haven't done anything."

Mark's booming voice filtered in. "Yes ,you did. You forced my patient in my own hospital into a sexual relationship."

He walked in with other orderlies. They grabbed Annika stood her up and led her away.

"It was consensual."

"Doesn't matter. She was a patient."

Paul's eye began to tear. "This is just like you. The minute I find something that makes me happy, you and your "morals" and "ethics" comes right on in to take it away. You've never been a real brother to me." He hissed acidly.

The police lead him handcuffed down the hall. He saw the orderlies taking Annika to a hospital room. At the moment their eyes met she began to rock back and forth.

"Where are you going Paul? Where are they taking you? You didn't hurt me....Let him go...let me go. "

She began to fight and the orderlies forced her into the patient room. Mark walked in the room and pulled out a shot of Thorazine. He closed the door behind him.

"Fuck you FLINT! FUCK YOU TO HELL!"

## 14

Lisa stood when an orange-suited Paul walked into the holding cell conference room.

She hugged him. "How are you holding up?"

"I'm alright. How's Annika?"

"She's fine. Mark gave her something to calm her down."

Paul sighed.

"I have some news. They are letting Mitch go."

"Why?"

"Annika refuses to press charges, since she is able to speak for herself, the judge let her decide. That means you will be free to go in a few hours."

"So she makes herself to be a flirtatious psycho to save my ass."

"That's not all. Mark spoke in court too, and you and Mitch are on a restraining order to stay away from her for 6 months."

"That son of a bitch."

Lisa looked grim. "She's pregnant, Paul."

Paul stared at Lisa until the tears fell.

"I'm sorry, Paul."

"It's mine, isn't it?

"Yes."

"Then I should be able to see her and be with her to have some kind of way to take care of this child."

"Mark doesn't think that's wise right now. You don't have a job."

"That piece of shit. He fired me?"

"Well, yes. Carol's gone too."

"Oh way to go Mark, three for three."

"Tell me what he should have done?"

Paul threw the file off the desk. "I expected him to understand that Annika and I are grown adults and the relationship just happened."

"She was a patient, Paul. Do you love her?"

He fell back in the chair and covered his eyes. 'Yes, I do."

Lisa got up to gather the papers. "A baby is a big responsibility."

"I know that."

"Are you sure you know that, Paul?"

He looked at her. "I would have damn well tried."

She sighed. "For what it's worth, I believe you."

Lisa stood up, stretched, and walked around the table to his side. He couldn't look at her, but she knew he was hurting.

"I'll talk to Mark."

'He seems sincere, Mark, I think he really does love her." Lisa hated playing middle man between Paul and Mark and this time was the worst it's ever been. They never got a chance to unwind in their bedroom late at night.

"Paul has no concept of love and commitment." Mark pulled his t-shirt off.

"But you think he'd really hurt Annika?"

"She's pregnant and back in the psychiatric ward on suicide watch. You tell me."

Lisa winced at the truth in his words. "She doesn't want an abortion."

"Nope, she's "in love" with him and wants to have her abuser's baby."

Lisa walked into the bathroom with him before he walked into the shower.

"You think he's abusive?"

"He's clearly a covert opportunist abuser."

"He's your brother. And what are you going to do with a pregnant woman in your psych ward?"

"Mom."

"Your mom?"

"Mom wants to take her and the baby in."

"Well, what about Paul?"

"What about him?

"Where's he going to live?"

"I have no clue." He turned the water on in the shower.

"HEY! FLINT. This doesn't sound like you at all. Paul needs to be an active part of the child's life and he's currently on a restraining order."

Mark stuck his head out the stall.

"You want to keep talking about this?"

"Uh yes, Flint. This is something that needs resolution."

"Well, you're going to have to get naked and get in here with me. This hot body won't scrub itself."

She rolled her eyes. "Okay, Flint, but you owe me big time." She took her shirt off and dropped her panties.

Mark looked down at her in the steam. "I'm glad I have you through all this."

"Not going to get all lovey dovey on me, are you?" She smiled.

"I might." He pulled her into his body.

She continued the talk on his chest in the darkness later that night.

"So what are we going to do?"

"Probably end up raising another child."

Lisa sighed. "Not that I have a problem with that, but I think Annika would be a great mother if she had some stability."

"She doesn't have stability, she has Paul. I'm sorry, but I don't trust him with her."

"You know, sometimes, you sound like Annika is your sister and Paul is not your brother.

"Feels that way sometimes. But Annika is just another mess I am cleaning up."

"Maybe we should give them a chance."

Mark didn't respond. "I was going to get Paul transferred to another part of the hospital; but now that I think about it. I think I should just let him flounder."

"Why wouldn't you help him?"

Mark sat up and turned on the light.

"Because Lisa, all we ever do is help him. He's never clamored to make anything work for him. I think the restraining order is a good idea. It would tell me if he's willing to stick it out with Annika and get a family together or if he runs away."

Lisa sat up. "I hate to say it, but I agree with you."

Mark looked at her and grinned. "You need to put some clothes on."

She fell back on the bed. "What's the point, they end up on the floor every night."

He laughed and turned off the light.

## 15

"Han encontrado Annika Garcia?" "Have you found Annika Garcia?"

General Montoya sat behind his desk with Sergeant Santos and a private giving a briefing on rounding up the last of the real witnesses of the failed coup that took place in his country in 2009.

The current government was still together but only by a thread. He had plans of his own to take over the country, but before he could act on that, he had to erase his involvement in that coup that did not give him the power he wanted. He wanted to be president. Micheletti managed to make himself the president and then essentially the dictator. He had lost his chance to take control. Now he had to erase all the evidence and this Annika Garcia, Honduras Embassy Interpreter was the last thread connecting him to Zelaya and Micheletti.

"We have come across something that might be of interest." "Nos hemos encontrado algo que puede ser de interés". The private pulled his tablet out and played a youtube video of a news report from the East Coast of the United States.

"Now, tonight, a young woman, a patient at Ashboro Psychiatric Hospital, was attacked by a security guard and another hospital staff member." The news report flashed Annika's face. The news woman described that the young woman was a patient that had been discharged working with the hospital when the attack had occurred.

"That's her. Where is the hospital?" Esa es ella. ¿Dónde está el hospital?"

"Ashboro Psychiatric is located in Knoxville, TN."
"Asheboro Psiquiátrica se encuentra en Knoxville, TN."

"How did a Honduras interpreter located in Washington DC get into a Knoxville, Tennessee?" "¿Cómo llegó un intérprete de Honduras localizado en Washington DC en un Knoxville, Tennessee?"

"Her father was an aristocrat that Zelaya had stolen everything. He wanted Annika for an escort but she was educated and a useful tool to him, so it never progressed to that. But when it seemed like he was going to be ousted, he "sold" her to a private American supporter. He must have put her in a mental institution. However, she never displayed unstable mental tendencies."

"Annika para una escolta, pero ella fue educada y una herramienta útil para él, por lo que nunca progresó a eso. Pero cuando parecía que iba a ser expulsado, la "vendió" a un partidario estadounidense privado. Debe haberla puesto en una institución mental. Sin embargo, nunca mostró tendencias mentales inestables."

The General sat up. "Her mental state is of no consequence. We need her back here and terminated." "Su estado mental no tiene ninguna consecuencia. La necesitamos aquí y terminó."

"-¿Por qué no terminarla en Estados Unidos? "Why not terminate her in the US?"

"Aquello podría funcionar." "That might work."

The two men looked at each other.

"But bring back a finger or her head for proof." "Pero trae un dedo o la cabeza para que pruebe." The General added. "Contact the US ambassador and insist that she is a criminal and finish this." "Póngase en contacto con la embajadora de Estados Unidos e insista en que es un criminal y termine esto".

Si senor. "Yes, sir.

"Te irás mañana. Tienes 73 horas para terminar esta misión o enviamos a otros hombres y todos termináis. ¿Tú entiendes? No deje testigos. Ni siquiera los estadounidenses que se interponen en el camino." "You leave tomorrow. You have 73 hours to finish this mission or we send other men and you all are terminated. You understand? Leave no witnesses. Not even Americans who get in the way."

They nodded in agreement.


Mark sat down across from Annika. He tried to temper his frustration that he knew would hurt her about Paul. Her fragility stood out and it concerned him. 'Damn you, Paul.' He thought. "And the poor girl loves him." He rolled his eyes.

"So how do you feel about everything?"

"I don't know."

Mark sighed "That's understandable.

"Where's Paul?"

"I haven't talked to him. My guess is that he's getting another job. He needs to pay his bills. With what's been going on I can't let you stay here and more. However, my mother as requested to let you move in with her until you figure out what you want to do."

"Why does she want to help me?"

"She wants to make sure that Paul's child is raised right."

"Oh." Annika felt confused.

"Everything will be A ok. We'll look after you. I need to get discharge papers ready. Then Lisa mom and I will come and help you get your things together. And we'll get you settled in."

"OK. Will I get to see Paul?"

"No. he's still under a restraining order for six months. He has to stay away from you for that long."

"Okay."

"Are you still considering keeping the baby?"

Annika shifted in her chair uncomfortably. "Yes."

Mark stood up. "Welcome to the family." He said smiling.

## 16

Paul thought it would be weeks before he could get a new job but a friend of his recommended him to be a firefighter that their local fire station. He went off for four weeks training. It didn't help to get Annika of his mind. He realized he was just biding his time until the six months were up and he could be with his family. Ha had already decided that he would commit to Annika and their coming baby and make this work.

He began the firefighting training while working fulltime at the station. His grades and of performance were top of the line and he made lieutenant in little over 4 weeks. He still found himself gazing into brown eyes and blonde hair every so often.

"Mr Flint could you come up to the front of the class and help me demonstrate the speed of how fire can spread in less than 60 seconds?" His instructor broke his daydream cruelly.

"Sure." He got up from his desk and walked up to te instructor's side. He held the matches as the teacher explained the process of air feeding fire and creating suffocating smoke.

He looked in the class and saw Annika again. He absently lighted the match and stared at the flame. His mind fixed on her eyes and not until the match burned him did he wake up and then drop the lighted match in a cup of kerosene.

BOOM! The fire popped out loud. The instructor poured water on the fire.

"What were you thinking, FLINT?"

He fidgeted slightly. "Uh, a girl."

The instructor rolled his eyes. "If you're not going to stop thinking about tits do keep yourself away from fire."

The class laughed. "Sit back down, Flint."

He walked to his seat and sat back down. Annika consumed his soul every day.

After days like this, he hadn't spoken with anyone in his family and certainly not Mark since Mark separated them from being together. The anger kept him up at night. His friend helped him keep it in check.

"Hey Mark, you staying overnight tonight at the fire station this weekend?"

"No. I'm going to go look at houses."

"What for?"

"Me and my girl are getting married and having a kid. I want a nice place for them to live."

"With a firefighter's salary?"

"Oh, I saved some money with my last job and invested it."

"That was smart."

"Yeah, I feel like I'm making better choices."

"Maybe love does that. But chicks go crazy after they get a ring and get married."

"Well, my girl is already crazy and I like that about her."

His friend laughed. "Good in bed?"

"Hot. You have no idea."

"Let me know if you break up."

Paul laughed. "Not a chance."

Former US Ambassador Carl Johnson growled in frustration when his wife mentioned the phone call from Honduras asked if he would meet with some military officials seeking information on reacquainting US and Honduran relationship for trade. He had been out of the political world for years and at 73, he and his wife had little use for the Washington scene. The US and Central American countries still courted a love hate relationship since the ousting of Noriega.

He researched the current state of affairs and everything seemed to have calmed down after the country succumbed to the military coup and ousting back in 2009. Michelletti took over and even he was removed from office. The military and the government were weak against the drug cartels looking for a free passage from drug infested countries in South America to Mexico and the United States. From what this message said was that a General in Honduras wanted aid and support for these fights against the cartel.

'Or could just want free money' he thought. The people of the country live with crime every day. It's not uncommon for rogue military looking to gain power and some money on the side. The US wouldn't back another Central America military general after the Noriega fiasco.

"I'll just tell them I'm retired and do not represent the United States government in Central America anymore. I'll point them to the State department here in Washington." He noticed they were planning to meet him at his home office at 2pm the next day.

Martha Flint loved having Annika in her home. She made herself useful cooking, cleaning, and tidying up the house. With Mark and Paul, she was the one that picked up after the boys.

"Annika, come here. I want to show you some pictures."

With her little belly protruding from her shirt, she came from the kitchen after washing dishes. "Yes, Miss Martha?"

"I pulled out some photos of the guys when they were little boys and I wanted to show you what you and Paul's baby might look like when he comes."

"You think it's a boy?"

"I have my own gut feelings on the matter. I'd love to have another granddaughter so I am not worried either way, but yes, I think you are having a boy."

Annika came and sat by Martha while she thumbed through the photo books. Mark and Paul stared up at them from the old pictures from old birthday parties and honors awards from grade school functions.

"So who was the best behaved?

Martha laughed. "That would be Mark, of course. I spoiled Pauley at a young age so he grew to be more of a challenge. But both boys were really smart. When their father left, Pauley fell right in step with Mark."

Annika looked at childhood some midget football and baseball photos. Except for differences in size, both boys wore the same jersey and they both had the same crooked smile. Paul's pictures were a bit more goofy. She smiled at his happy face.

"Did they fight much? Get jealous?"

"Before their father left, yes, but after he left, they seemed to work together to help me. I was a fulltime veterinarian doctor and worked many hours. Mark kept Paul and Paul secretly idolized Mark. He did everything Mark did. Then Paul hit puberty, found out about girls and the party never ended."

Annika looked up at her face. "Does Paul disappoint you?"

Martha heaved a great sigh. "Yes, and no. The boy can do or be anything. Quick learner. Good with people. He just doesn't believe it himself."

"What's he doing now? Have you talked to him?"

"Yes. He's become a firefighter. And a good one. Just like always."

Annika smiled. Paul really did have this magic quality to him to make things work. She hoped against hope that he loved her and their baby.

Martha looked in her face and read her thoughts. "I'll talk to Paul and see if he has a message he wants to send you. He's keeping the terms of the restraining order so he can get another chance to do everything right this time. You have been a good influence on him."

"You are very sweet. But I doubt I did anything special."

Martha smiled and put an arm around her. "Yes, you did Annie. He's never been in love before."

## 17

Sergeant Santos and his private entered the United States without any trouble as official Honduran representatives set up by General Montoya. They had no problem acquiring a car and finding the ambassador's Washington house. The ambassador couldn't hide his displeasure of being visited by people he'd thought he'd never have to deal with again. These Central and South American people were sleezy with their money and drug ties. He was glad he didn't have to deal with 'these people' anymore so having to help these men was unsavory at best.

"How can I help you gentlemen?"

"We are here looking for someone."

Their broken English and thick Spanish accent was an immediate red flag.

"We are here looking for political dissident. Here her name and picture."

The ambassador took the photo and read the name- Annika Garcia. He remembered her face clearly. She was a very bright and pretty Honduran interpreter that lived in DC. His younger brother had a thing for her. He had some papers about her that his brother left in his file cabinet.

"I might can help you. Give me a moment, gentlemen."

They nodded and watched him leave the room. About 10 minutes later, he emerged with a folder. "This was my brother's information. From what he told me, he was helping her get her green card to stay in America as a permanent UN interpreter. I haven't looked at this. He left it here years ago and forgot to pick it back up." He handed it to the men.

The private opened the folder and read the papers. He handed a few pages to General Santos. He looked and saw the documents of transferring a young women named Annika Garcia from Virginia psychiatric medical center to Ashboro Regional Psychiatric in Knoxville, TN. The papers mentioned that after a bad session with electro shock memory erasing, she began to have seizures and catatonic episodes.

The General looked at the private and then to the retired ambassador. "Thank you for your help. We will take this and leave immediately."

"Glad I could be of help, gentlemen."

The General and the private walked out of his house and to their car.

"We should leave no evidence we've been here."

The private nodded and pulled a gun with a silencer. He walked into the house and put a bullet in the heads of the retired ambassador and his wife. No one heard a single sound.

The maid discovered the bodies the next morning.

Annika rolled slowly out of bed, her belly protruding out and feeling awkward. Martha had agreed to take her to her doctor's visit scheduled at 11am. Waking up at 8 gave her 2 hours to gather enough strength to be alert during the visit. Being pregnant zapped her energy quickly at 6 months.

She walked downstairs to the kitchen where the smell of eggs and bacon hit her hard and her hunger clenched tight in her stomach. Martha noticed her tired face.

"How are you feeling today?"

Annika groaned.

Martha laughed. "That's how the Flint boys are. Take all your energy and your food. Then stomach gymnastics every night during Wheel of Fortune."

Annika grabbed the bowl of grits, eggs, and bacon and shoveled it into her mouth. "I like this white stuff…"

"Grits?"

"Yes…it's like warm love in my tummy."

Martha uproared with laughter. "Mark is coming over in an hour. I want to talk to him about you and Paul seeing each other again. He has about a month left on the restraining order. He's looking at a house for you and he."

"Wow."

"Yes, he's really changed everything around. We are so proud of him. We're hoping he keeps this streak going."

As they were they were talking, Mark knocked on the kitchen door. He missed the two men in a black Ford Focus watching the house across the street.

Paul was at fire station washing down some fire trucks talking it with his pal and a police officer discussing the latest football game stats. His friends were trying to entice Paul into their fantasy football league but he was resisting hard.

"Nah, Tom Brady is a bitch, man. He has to have his football 'soft' in order to throw a good pass? What the hell is that?"

"Yeah, well, I'm sick and tired of the Peyton Place brothers and their crap."

"Yes, but they are a family of talent. At least you don't hear them trying to fix a game in their favor. Just pathetic!" Paul sprayed the fire truck down with a playful slap.

The cop friend laughed and reached into his car after hearing a buzz from the station. He reached down and listen to his CB. He yelled out to Paul. "Hey! I have to go…Doesn't your mom live on 297 Clayton Road?"

Paul dropped the water hose. "Yeah!"

"There's been a home invasion, a woman calling about two men trying to take her. A man has been shot and an elderly woman knocked out. The phone went dead before she mentioned a black car."

'Annika!' His mind exploded. Paul, with his firemen outfit, ran to his jeep.

"Wait, Paul!"

"Follow me, I can get there quickly!"

"We'll need backup."

"Fuck backup!"

He started the jeep and sped off. His friend jumped in his car and followed him but Paul was almost out of site.

Paul pulled up in his mother's yard. He saw Mark shot in the upper chest on the ground.

"Mark! Mark talk to me. Come on….Stay with me."

Mark moaned and blood poured out of his wound. The cop drove up while Paul chatted with Mark keeping him awake. Tears poured out of Paul's eyes.

"Mark, Did you see Annika, did you see the men? What happened

"No." He whispered. "Saw car. Black. Drove east. Go."

The cop ran up to Mark. "Dr. Flint, the ambulance is coming. I'm going to check for Mrs. Flint."

"Paul. Go…get…her. They'll…kill her."

Paul looked up and heard the sirens and the ambulance.

"I'll talk to Lisa while I drive."

Mark grabbed his hand. "Love you, Pauley."

"Stay alive, Mark." He kissed his head.

Paul ran back to his jeep. He knew he didn't have a chance. 'God, I need You right now'. The jeep peeled out and sped down the road after a black Ford Focus. He dialed Lisa to tell her of the crime.

"LISA!"

Paul heard her answer her phone. She was already hysterical in her car headed to the hospital.

"PAUL!"

"Lisa, I need you to breathe, but I saw Mark.....he's alive. I didn't see Mom, but she only had a knock on her head."

"Paul, Paul, Paul, how did this happen?"

"I don't know. Mark told me to look for the black car, I'm on the road."

"Be careful, Paul. I was always worried Annika had a past."

"What do you mean?"

"She's Honduran. She was an interpreter during the 2009 coup."

"So these guys are from Central America?"

"Yes. They are dangerous."

"Ok."

"You need to let the authorities handle this."

"Lisa, they're not here kidnapping, they are here to kill her. I have to go." He hung up.

"Paul…" The phone went dead. "Lord, I hope you aren't in over your head!" She fought hysterics.

He zoomed east on the connecting freeway going 90 miles per hour. The mountain turns were dangerous but he had experience driving the Blue Ridge Mountains. He knew the kidnappers didn't and it worked in his favor. Within 20 minutes, he'd caught up with them driving slow and careful not trying to attract attention to themselves.

Paul charged up and knocked their bumper and their car veered into the ditch. They careened left and stalled. He parked and ran to the car. He saw Annika passed out in the back. He opened the front door and punched the Honduran private and pulled his gun and shot the sergeant in the arm. While they scrambled in the car, Paul opened the backseat and grabbed Annika and dragged her from the car. The sergeant started the car and spun wheels trying to get out of the ditch. He carried her to his jeep. He jumped in, started the car, and turned around back to Knoxville.

He saw the Honduran killers pull out of the ditch and raced up behind him. The Hondurans began shooting at them and Paul swung off on a dirt mountain road with them following him closely.

Barrett Farm Road went deep into the mountains and climbed high up to give tourists impressive views of the Blue Ridge and the Smoky Mountains. Paul knew he could drive up on a fork off this road and hide from people who were looking for him. He brought dates up here to make out sessions in order to be alone and undisturbed. He found it ironic that he would be bringing his future wife up here to save his and her life. He found the off road path and climbed up to the cliff overlook and shut off his jeep. He was running low on gas and he knew he had no chance to outrun them without getting to a gas station.

He looked at Annika. She had a goose egg bruise on her forehead and rug burns on her pregnant belly. He quietly examined her and noticed blood in her shorts.

"Dammit!"

She began to come out of her haze. Paul put a hand over her mouth. "Shhh. We're hiding."

She put her arms around him and he held her tenderly.

The Hondurans turned the car around and headed back to the main highway. They had lost the Americans on an unfamiliar back mountain road.

"General Montoya will not be happy that we lost her."

"I know."

They crept along the road slowly. They drove gingerly around sharp mountains turns when a disturbance caught their eyes. A Jeep parked above them lurched unleashing a rock slide on their car.

Paul was sitting there holding Annika when the dirt under the jeep slipped and fell down the trail. He heard a car turn and charge up the road with the driver and passenger pulling out their guns and shooting them.

"Shit! Annika get down!" He pushed her in the floorboard and turned his jeep on. He pulled out and slammed into the Ford Focus. The men in the Ford Focus kept shooting. He pushed the Ford back to the dirt road. With one more push, he pushed the car over the sharp cliff and it rolled down the steep incline down into the deep valley.

He felt a wet warm ooze slide down his arm. He'd been shot. The pain began to course through his left arm and pound into his brain. He drove them back to Knoxville and to Ashboro Medical Center. He, Annika, his mother, and brother were in the same ICU.

## 18

Paul and his mother were treated and released later that day. Paul's arm was grazed by a bullet but nothing more than a flesh wound. His mother had a lump on her forehead but it was not serious with no sign of a concussion. They went home to rest for the night leaving Lisa and the kids in the emergency waiting room. Mark took a bullet to the upper chest an inch away from his heart. The doctors put him in a coma to regulate shock and promote healing. Paul was back up at the hospital with Annika. She was stable and the Ob-Gyn was confident that she wouldn't go into labor early and lose the baby.

"I'm putting you on bed rest for the next 3 months. If you should go into labor get to the emergency room immediately."

"Yes, Doctor."

The doctor looked at Paul severely. "You need to be sure there aren't any more exciting events between now and the baby's birth."

"Yes, ma'am."

They discharged Annika and Paul took her to his place. He wasn't taking any chances with losing her or their baby.

He decided to visit Mark and Lisa later that night. The FBI met him in the waiting room to question him on the shooting and the possible connection between the ambassador and his wife's double murder in DC.

"We did a search, Mr. Flint and we found that the same Ford Focus that is pictured outside of the retired Ambassador's house matched the same vehicle that attacked your mother and your fiancé. Did you see the killers when you chased down the car?"

"Yes, a young Hispanic and an older Hispanic. I caught up to them and was able to get Annika away from them. They pursued me and followed me up a mountain road and they fell off the side of the road down to the Barrett Farm beneath."

"Fell off the road, huh? Dr. Lisa told us everything she had investigated on Annika Garcia and the relationship between her and Honduran executioners. We'll get in touch with the State Department on the details. We'll issue your fiancé a temporary green card. We may need her personal testimony on this situation."

"Yes. We understand."

"Keep in touch, Mr. Flint."

He nodded at the investigators. He walked into the ER and saw Lisa sitting in Mark's room.

"Hey." She stood up and put her arms around him. "How are you?"

"I'm ok. How's Mark?"

"He's better. They brought him out of a coma. He's dozing now. Doctor says he'll be here for another 2 weeks if he cooperates."

"Haha, big Mark will push for one week."

"I've already had to start bribing him. Hey, I need to get something to eat, you mind staying with him?"

"Sure."

She kissed his cheek. "Don't let him talk you into anything."

Paul laughed and sat down.

After 5 silent minutes, Mark spoke to Paul in a weak voice.

"Pauley?"

Paul stood up and walked to him. "Yeah, big guy?"

"Can you….go and …..get me my….."

He grabbed his hand. "Tell me, Markee."

"I'm jonesing for…

"Yes, yes…" Paul prodded.  He leaned in closer.

"A whopper from Burger King."

Paul rolled his eyes. "You know you can't eat that.

"Lisa's killing me with the hospital food."

"Doctors make the worst patients.'

"Yes, well, I am much better. The bullet went through and I won't need surgery."

"That's good."

"So I heard you got Annika back. That's pretty good hero work, Paul."

"I didn't think I just did it."

"So she's good, she and the baby?"

"Yes. Tell me what happened at mom's house?"

"I came in the back door to the kitchen. I noticed the car parked across the road but thought it was the neighbor's visitor or something. They were in there eating when I went upstairs to look for something. I heard Mom scream and I raced back down, saw two men knock mom out and dragging Annika out the front door. I ran back up was going to grab her and then punch but one of them shot me point blank. They drove off and like a second later you were there."

Paul's eyes teared up after hearing the story. "I've been a mess with all of us, haven't I?"

Mark sighed. "You've changed a lot Paul."

"Well, at least I helped this time."

"You did."

Mark and Paul hugged each other.

"No one can defeat the Flint brothers." Paul laughed wiping the tears from his eyes.

Mark smiled. "No one."